The War Lord

Virginia C. Holmgren

The War Lord

Illustrations by Dan Siculan

FOLLETT PUBLISHING COMPANY

Chicago   **F**   *New York*

Library of Congress Catalog Card Number: 70-85155

SBN 695-89176-6   Trade
SBN 695-49176-8   Titan

First Printing I

TO MY HUSBAND

who has shared with me many a journey
and homecoming in lands near and far
and who has also shared my pleasure in learning
to know the pheasants
who nest on our Oregon hillside

Except for Owen Denny and his family and the historical facts of their sending the first Chinese ring-necked pheasants to breed successfully in North America, the characters and incidents in this book are wholly fictitious, but based on a thorough study of pheasant behavior.

PART I

THE WAR LORD AND THE JOURNEY

Shanghai to Oregon, January to July, 1882

1

On the riverbank beyond Shanghai's western wall, where scraggly thickets were bleak and winter bare beside the stubble fields, a ringnecked pheasant paused with wary glance. Slowly he moved his head to survey the weedy tangle that Farmer Wah Lo had left standing at the field's edge.

The crimson cheek armor on the turning head was not quite so gaudy as it had been in springtime courtship, the blue-black feather plumicorns on his crown not quite so alertly lifted in conscious splendor, but he was splendid enough. This was his world; his to defend against all enemies; his to guard for mates and young. Now in midwinter the poults were full grown, and he recognized no hen as mate, but both his former mates and the summer's broods of young hens and cockerels were in his loosely united flock. They fed in his terrain and gave him due homage as the largest, wisest, most fiercely belligerent rooster in the band. It took wisdom and belligerence to lead a flock—or even see to one's own livelihood—in a world where enemies might come at any moment, on foot or wing. And there were also those inescapable enemies that came each winter: cold and hunger.

The cock was hungry now, and here before him was an unexpected dribble of grain beside the weed-tangled thorn bush. But he was no foolish poult to eat without caution. He looked to the right, to the left, testing the air, listening for the betraying rustle of some enemy lurking behind the weed-grown screen. He could not hear danger, nor see it, but still some undefinable sense gave warning, and he waited motionless, bright feathers suddenly blending with earth and grass and dark thrusting branch, sunlight dappled with shadow.

Between the plumicorns, his crown feathers were pale green-gold. Throat and nape were a shimmer of deep midnight blue, jeweled with a sapphire and emerald iridescence that marked pheasant kinship with the peafowl. Below the peacock hues and the shining circle of the white torque that gave the ringnecks their name, his breast feathers were richly bronze and gold touched with jet, and on wings and back and sweeping tail plumes were all the radiant colors that glow on a mandarin's silk embroidered robe or from a Manchu emperor's opened jewel chest.

Farmer Wah Lo, watching hopefully from behind

the thorn bush, was not thinking of the cock's jewel-and-treasure tones. He was thinking of the high price that the American consul-general in Shanghai would pay for pheasants brought to him before sundown. Ordinarily this big cock was too wise to be fooled by a baited net, but the weather had been cold of late and food scarce. Hunger might well get the better of his wisdom. Just let him take one more step forward, take one peck at the grain, and Wah Lo would let the net fall.

His fingers on the jerk-string were cramping now, but he willed them to stay ready for quick action. The cock had to be taken within minutes or not at all. When the American consul Owen Denny said "Before sundown," he meant it. This was the last day that he would pay his high price for good healthy pheasants alive and unharmed. Seven captive hens were already in the big round basket of woven cane awaiting this promised fee, and Wah Lo was sure that he could get twice that for the cock.

If only the bird would take that final step, and take it now. The Honorable Consul Denny had made it very clear that he would not wait past the sunset hour. Americans were always in a hurry, of course, but this time there was good reason. The Consul and his lady were buying these pheasants to send to their home-

13

land—a place called Oregon—and the ship was ready to sail this very day. No other ship would do, because this was the only one going straight to a port where the Consul's brother would be waiting to take them in charge.

The cook at the consulate was a friend of Wah Lo's and had explained it all very carefully. There were no pheasants in Oregon or in all America! No ringnecks, no goldens, no silvers. No wild pheasants of any kind. That was why the Consul was willing to pay such a high price to get them. These birds were to be the ancestors for a whole new clan of American-born pheasants. The Consul had tried to send pheasants to America before, but the birds had all died, for some reason.

Wah Lo, eyes still glued on the cock, thought he knew what had happened. Except right now in mid-winter, no cock would allow another rooster to share a shipping crate with him and a flock of hens. Oh, but these ringnecks could be fierce warriors in spring when they battled for the hens. Wah Lo chuckled silently, with the understanding of one male for another. A pheasant cock was no bird to be satisfied with a single mate. Like any emperor or man of wealth, this lordly creature relished a full court of respectful and obedient wives. Even an ordinary

14

pheasant rooster would claim two or three hens, and a big handsome fellow like this one would demand every hen in sight, fight each rival to turntail defeat or to the death.

Oh, yes, he could understand why the Consul was in a hurry to get his pheasant ancestors aboard ship and—

Suddenly the cock was stepping forward, bending to the grain with hunger's rat-tat beat. Wah Lo's fingers twitched in exultant response and the net fell with a soft, hissing rustle. He sprang forward to bind the bird's wings fast, lest one gleaming feather be set awry to lessen its value. Quickly he slipped this new captive into the basket with the hens and was on his way to the harbor, grinning over his shoulder at the westering sun. He had waited longer than was wise, risking a win-all, lose-all gamble for this special cock. But wasn't life worthless without gamble and risk? he asked himself, jauntily sure of the answer now that he had won. The Honorable Consul Denny would surely pay double for a bird like this. No yearling short-spur, this fellow. He was a seasoned battler, a—a—

A veritable War Lord. Yes, that was the fitting title. War Lord.

2

Down at Shanghai dockside, the barque *Isle of Bute* was nearly ready to sail. Consul Owen Nickerson Denny and his wife Gertrude Jane were both on hand to make final check of the special bamboo enclosure that had been built amidships for this hopeful cargo. It was a huge cage twenty feet high and twenty feet wide, and a whole scowload of gravel had been towed out and spread on the cage floor to give the birds grit scratch and dusting place, for good health's sake. Sacks of grain were stored nearby, and the *Bute* crew had been paid well to tend to their feathered passengers. Within the cage a small forest of tubbed bamboo seedlings and young fruit trees and other plants stood round about to give the birds both the needed daily ration of greens in their diet and a familiar background. Perhaps this green camouflage would trick the birds into accepting the bars this time, Owen thought hopefully.

The ringneck's yearning for freedom was a factor that he had learned from the failure of his first venture

16

in pheasant transplantation. The barque *Otago*, that had carried his first shipment a year ago, had docked at Port Townsend, Washington, some miles up the coast from their Oregon destination. No one had foreseen any trouble in transferring them to smaller crates for shipping down to Portland. But with one glimpse of good earth and free sky, the birds had gone wild, battering themselves to death against the bars, willing to give life for hope of liberty.

Perhaps he should have chosen golden pheasants or silvers, as some of his Chinese friends had suggested. They were more biddable birds than the ringnecks, took more willingly to caging. But a docile cage bird for zoo or aviary was not what he and Gertrude had in mind for their Oregon homeland. That day when they had first seen the ringnecks in their courtyard—bold, beautiful, and defiant even in captivity—they had both been struck with an unshakable desire to see these birds claiming wild heritage in Oregon's green fields and glens.

To others, they had tried to give their impulse practical explanation. Native northwest gamebirds were on the decline. One had to hunt hard for a bag of swans, geese, ducks, or grouse these days, and the market-hunters usually beat others to it, taking birds to ship by the barrel to Seattle, Portland—even San

17

Francisco. Oregon needed a gamebird sturdy and cunning enough to outwit the market-hunters, and what likelier candidate than the ringneck?

But first Owen had to get enough birds to Oregon for a fair start. Last year, only seventeen ringnecks—three hens and fourteen cocks—had survived the battle against the bars to be set free at Sauvie Island in the Columbia River on the farm of his friend George Green. None of them had been seen for months now, and the seven Chefoo partridges and eleven sand grouse he'd sent along had vanished also. Well, he'd added a few partridges this time, too—as well as fine breeds of geese and ducks for his brother's poultry yard. But it was the ringnecks that carried his high hopes.

"This time they'll make it," Gertrude said, reading his thoughts as usual.

Denny nodded, his spirits rising as they always did at her enthusiasm. Then he saw Wah Lo coming aboard with a full basket—seven hens and one cock—and his spirits rose still higher. Hens were what he needed. In that first batch, the three hens just hadn't been enough, and the surplus cocks had turned wanderers—as they always did when denied mates—searching so single-mindedly for the hens that they grew careless of their own safety. Now he'd have two

18

mates for every cock—if all survived the voyage—for there were nine cocks and twelve or more hens already in the big coop.

"Here you are," he beckoned the farmer, counting out the promised sum, and was surprised to see the man shake his head, asking double fee for the big cock, giving it some special praise.

"What did he say?" Gertrude asked, and the cook —who had come along as master of transactions— gave a grinning interpretation.

"War Lord. Strong and powerful, like War Lord. Very worthy ancestor. Worth twice as much as hen."

"Well, I don't know about that!" she bristled in ready defense of feminine rights. But one look at the cock and she capitulated. "Please pay what he asks, Owen. That cock is a beauty."

Owen counted out the coins, not missing the grin that went from farmer to cook to jingling wealth— wealth in which the cook would have his backhand share, of course. But he told Gertrude that the hens were worth double money in this pioneer venture, not the cocks. The hens lacked the bright feathers, but they were the ones who would rear the first American-born chicks and give the cocks family responsibilities to keep them on guard against pheasant foes.

"John will help," Gertrude said reassuringly.

Denny nodded. His brother John and the rest of the family and all their Linn County neighbors would help this second time, for the birds were to be released near the Denny homestead. He wished he'd had time to gather more than the scant thirty birds, but the *Isle of Bute* could not wait. Neither could the pheasants. As it was, the barque would not make the seven-week crossing before mid-March, and by then the cocks might already be showing courtship belligerence, ready to kill each other for the hens' favor. Even now that last big cock looked as if he were ready to do battle for flock leadership.

"Kruk, kkrrrrkk!" He was giving arrogant command, forcing the others to cede him first rights at the scattered grain. Now he shook himself like a wet dog till every feather stood out at straight angle, making him seem twice size, and beneath his gleaming garnet stare the others backed away, offering small protest.

"War Lord is right!" Gertrude chuckled. "I don't wonder that Jason and the Argonauts thought these birds were worth bringing back from the Land of the Golden Fleece."

Her history was not quite accurate. It was the blackneck pheasant—close cousin and almost exact duplicate of the ringneck except for the white collar— that the Argonauts or some other Greek adventurers had found. Jason's role might be unprovable myth, but the ancient Greek records were explicit in describing the birds and locating their origin. They had been found on the far shore of the Black Sea, in the province then called Colchis, along the banks of the river Phasis. Greek scholars had promptly named them *Phasianos ornis*—the Phasian birds—and with this name they had been carried by the Romans to all the European lands where the conquering legions made settled outposts—even to England. English colonists in America had tried to establish blackneck broods, but every one had failed. Yet the ringnecks were known across China, north to Manchuria, Korea, and Japan, south to the Gulf of Tonkin. Ringnecks were being painted on Chinese scrolls and porcelains two thousand years before Christ—and that was a thousand years before the blacknecks were portrayed on any Grecian urn, so Gertrude had been told by Shanghai scholars.

"They'll make good this time," she said. "We'll have our American pheasants. Oh. Owen, do you think they'll name them Denny pheasants—after you?"

Owen shrugged a disclaimer, explaining that the birds were already enrolled under one Latin label on scientific lists, and one name was all that was allowed under the system started by the great Swedish classi-

21

fier Carl Linnaeus, a system followed since 1758 by scientists all around the world. Linnaeus himself had classified the blackneck, but the ringnecked pheasant had been identified, described, and christened some thirty years later by the German naturalist Gmelin, who undertook to revise and add to the listings after Linnaeus's death. *Phasianus colchicus torquatus* was the official listing—Phasian bird from Colchis with the white neck ring.

"Humph!" Gertrude challenged. "Who's going to call them that—in Oregon?"

Her husband's grin admitted that she had made a point; then his lips tightened. "I don't care what they call them," he said earnestly, "just so long as they let them alone for awhile. Give them a chance to settle down and raise a brood or two before the shootists get after them."

"Shootist" was Denny's own word for any gunner with too ready a trigger finger—anyone who killed deer, elk, or gamebird just to be killing, without any real pleasure in the outdoorsman's world of field and stream, pungent pine forest, high mountain lake, and snowcapped peaks. Pot hunters at least had the excuse of hunting to fill their own empty bellies, but some of them could be "shootists" too, tossing first-taken prey of squirrel or rabbit to the dogs or dung heap whenever some tastier morsel came in range—swan or crane, a nice plump Canada honker, or some canvasbacks. And now there would be pheasants, also, to add to the favored list. He couldn't imagine anyone who couldn't stir up a hankering for the taste of a pheasant's tender breast meat, once he'd had a chance to try it. Or how could anyone fail to enjoy the beauty of that gorgeous plumage?

"They just have to make it, this time," he said.

He fairly ached with the intensity of his desire to see these jewel-bright cocks and soft-toned hens amid the green setting of Oregon woodlands and the round-hilled river valley where he himself had come pioneering with father, mother, brother, and sisters nearly thirty years ago. It had been September of 1852 when the Denny family had reached Oregon after an uneventful but wearying pioneer trek from Ohio in ox-drawn wagons. He'd been only fourteen then and when his father died just ten days after arrival, he'd learned what pioneering hardships could mean.

Gertrude had learned in even more harrowing ordeal, for she had lost her father in the terrible Whitman Mission massacre and she and her mother and baby sisters had been held captive for days. She didn't talk about those days, but she remembered them. More than once Denny had seen her start up, quivering, at unexpected burst of gunfire or at children's shouts that sounded like Indian warwhoop.

It occurred to him suddenly that the native birds might resent the pioneer pheasants, just as the Indians had resented the white settlers. But no—surely there was room for all. Of course there would be enemies— the same foes they found here—hawk, owl, flesh-eating animals of all kinds, snakes. In any land each wild thing had its prey and was prey in turn to something else. Bobcats killed pheasants and pheasants killed grasshoppers, spiders, crickets. But in the green plenty of Oregon, they would have more than fair chance of survival. And they would be free.

Denny wished that somehow he could tell these birds that freedom would be theirs at journey's end. He wished also that he could know—right now—if the ringnecks would find Oregon a welcome home. There was so much that could go wrong when unwitting wild things were set down on a pioneer trail not of their own choosing.

With one last glance at the bamboo cage, one last earnest wish for good journey and safe landfall, Owen turned away.

"Might as well go, I guess," he said to Gertrude. "We've done everything we can. The rest is up to luck."

"And up to the War Lord," Gertrude amended, giving the big cock an amused look over her shoulder. "I'd say he's ready to rule the roost right now."

The pheasant did not even turn his head as she spoke, or heed the rustle of their departure. Watchers that went away were none of his concern. What mattered now was that he make good his first claim to leadership of this strange, yet half familiar, domain. The first bold challenge had to be followed by vigilant reminders of his rank, a willingness to meet all contenders—or to so conduct himself that no contenders dared show spur.

Now he stretched himself to full-height survey, the white neck ring standing out like a royal collar of pearls or ermine against the velvet sheen of darker throat feathers, a sheen that flicked from sapphire to emerald and back again as each turn and twist caught a changing light to dance on the prism facets of each feather. He shook out his breast feathers, each one a gleaming arrow of gold, bronze, amber, then let them sink slowly back into accustomed smoothness as he lifted his wings, revealing the gray-blue rump patch that matched the gray-blue shoulder capes—blue plus blue, the coat-of-arms that marked his sub-clan lineage within the pheasant family group.

Every other cock in the cage had that same clan mark, and every one could have given as imperial a display—if they had felt the drive to declare their own right to leadership. Another time, another place, and the War Lord could well have had to prove his worth, but now he met no sign of defiance. Perhaps the other cocks had had rougher treatment by their captors, or longer imprisonment in the confining basket, and were still in a state of half shock. Perhaps they were uneasy at the strange motion beneath them as the barque slipped out on the tide and bowed to the ocean's heavier swells.

The War Lord sought no reason for the lack of challenge. He turned now from the cocks to the nearest hen—a calm and sturdy looking creature some two or three years old—and invited her to share the scattered grain before him, repeating the invitation with benevolent clucks. She hesitated—after all, there was plenty of the same grain all about her—but at the second summons she accepted obediently, moving over to eat at the spot he indicated with drumming beak. When she was pecking away in proper submission, he cast his eye upon a smaller hen and summoned her also. She half lifted one wing, as if she had mistaken his invitation for a threat, but as he churked again with more peremptory voice, she skittered across the heav-

26

ing deck and began to eat.

"Kkkrukk," said the War Lord in the tone reserved for pronouncement of royal satisfaction, and so the pact was sealed, his rule acknowledged. During the seven-week voyage he would not be challenged with more than half-hearted defiance. Indeed, few of the birds seemed to have more than half-hearted interest in anything. The shrinking of their world to this small, odd-shaped thicket of such unsteady footing was so out of keeping with their natural way of life that their whole pattern seemed at rest point, a prolonging of the winter hiatus that held them bound each year only by the needs of their own survival.

But it could not remain so much longer. The wind that now came to fill the barque's well-worn sails was from the southwest, heady with its hint of the lands where spring was already in full tilt. Yet the nights were cold, as March nights have a right to be off Oregon shores, and a sudden rain squall could bring a wintry reminder at any moment. The War Lord bowed his head to the rain, but yielded not so much as an inch to any rival.

3

On March 13, 1882, the *Isle of Bute* nosed down the winding Columbia River entry toward Portland docks. Amidships in their bamboo courtyard, the pheasants were still healthy and fairly tractable. Only two or three hens had died and the others were already showing springtime alertness. It was a good thing that John Denny was right on hand to meet them, for rivalry between the cocks could not be postponed much longer.

Just for safety's sake—to avoid curious visitors and those over-eager "shootists" Owen was always worrying about—John asked the newspaper reporters not to disclose the birds' destination. The *Oregonian* complied with a smugly cryptic passage in the March 19 paper, page one:

> Their habitat is known to us, but we suppress it for reasons that have a bearing upon the field shooting of the dulcet hereafter. Ten years from now no swell dinner will be complete without them, thanks to Judge Denny of Shanghai.

Yes, the pheasants were meant to be game birds,

he told eager questioners. But not now. Now their purpose was to become settled in Oregon, accept it as natural homeland, to grow strong and healthy themselves and produce sturdy young. There wasn't a one of them—except maybe the biggest cock—that didn't need fattening up before facing the pioneer venture.

Hopefully, John called on his son Malcolm and a visiting nephew to help him open the small shipping crates and turn the birds loose in the Denny chicken-yard. If only they would be content here a few days, eat well—

"Krrk!" challenged the big cock, coming from the crate at last. He had warned the others to wait and they had not obeyed him, had forgotten caution completely at sight of the grain on the ground, not noticing the wire enclosure. Now from among the feeding hens, one bold rooster stepped forward to defy the War Lord's right to command. As if on signal, the other birds drew away, and the two cocks began shifting weight from foot to foot, each eyeing the other. The truce was over.

Before the birds knew what was happening, three pairs of hands were reaching for them, scooping challenger and watching hens and cocks into separate crates—two hens with each of the first six roosters, then three cocks with only one hen each.

At the first move the War Lord had quickly rounded up three hens for himself, crowding them into a corner and taking a spread-wing guard with head atilt. Now, as a hand reached out toward him, he jabbed at it with telling blows, heard angry exclamations and then felt some heavy cloth fall over him and the hens. Then they were in the crate, carried on a stumbling journey over rough ground, up one side of a hill and down the other, then finally set down and the shrouding canvas taken away.

On the ground before the open crate was a familiar scattering of grain, but the War Lord did not stir. He had seen also the watching figures of the man and boy, and he would not move till they had gone. He heard the man say something, then turn away, the boy following, and when there was no longer echo or vibration of footfall, the cock at last stepped warily into the open.

But he would not yet let the hens come to feed. Strong within him, in clearer warning than he had known for weeks, came survival's tocsin: Take care! He was once again a wildling, with only instinct and self-taught cunning to outwit his enemies. And enemies were always at hand. Always. They came on four legs or two, on slinking belly and on wide wings. Earthborne or airborne, danger was always near. Only the wary survived. Only the wary could keep their wild freedom.

From deep within him the ringneck's instinct for claiming wild freehold surged upward. This land was his. He would take it, here, now.

He stepped forward, calling the hens to follow, spurning the captives' grain as he looked over his surroundings. There were trees, huge of trunk and limb, both fir and oak. There were tangled vines of wild rose and blackberry to give both cover and food— food even now when spring fruits had not yet formed, for the rose vines still held their winter-bounty of seed pods. Rose hips might not be the juiciest of fare, but at this season they were more than welcome. Small birds had already been feasting on them, leaving tell-tale marks.

He went on, stopping every few steps to look to the right, to the left, listening always. At a sudden rustle of scurrying feet on dead leaves, he whirled about to see a chipmunk take to quick heels, its tail a small furry spike of upright rufous indignation at this invasion of territory. Safe on a fir branch, it paused to sound a high-pitched *chee-chee-chee* of warning. Now a Steller's jay, bold in blue coat with slate-colored hood and crest, took up the alarm with raucous voice, but at sight of the War Lord's imposing bulk, it flew

31

off to shout its protests at a safer distance.

At the jay's repeated cry, a flock of Oregon juncoes swept up from the weed patch in a dot-dash pattern of white tail feathers and black hoods. A song sparrow cut off its bubbling warble in mid-trill, and from beneath a fern clump, two ruddy-brown fox sparrows stopped their both-feet-at-once scratching long enough to assay the danger that jay and chipmunk had proclaimed and then went back to work, seeing nothing in the strange, long-tailed bird to reckon as enemy. The juncoes, caught in the open, had been forced to fly first and assess the danger later, but the fox sparrows' arbor of dry brown fern fronds to match their coloring gave them protection for immobile survey.

The War Lord spied them out, even so, but he was used to sharing his fields with small brown birds—or small birds of any hue—and did not count them as rivals. Birds not of his own size, or those not taking the same food and nesting places that he and his hens would need, were none of his concern. What was his concern at this moment was a safe night roost, and so he sought the sort of cover in which he and his kind had slept without danger before. That was the pattern of his learning: what had served well would be chosen again. If he could not find such a place here, then he would search farther.

But he soon saw that there were roosting places in plenty, one for tonight and others for nights to come, for changing sleeping quarters was well-established pheasant custom. It was also custom to roost near water, so that pheasant thirst might easily be quenched each morning and evening, and now the War Lord looked for some sign of a nearby stream. If need be, he could satisfy his thirst with dew or raindrops caught in upturned leaf cups, but seeking a stream was another unquestioned part of his heritage. It was not his responsibility to figure out that wherever a river flowed there would be the banks of greenery and the buzzing insects that formed an important part in pheasant diet, as well as water. This was pheasant custom, and this was what he sought, and in a few moments he found it —a trickling stream that channeled through a wide gravel bed where a deeper river had once run. He drank, and the hens drank also, and then the four turned back to the glen, nibbling on whatever seed, grass tip, or bud looked inviting.

Every few steps they had to detour around the stump of an old Douglas fir left by cut-out-and-get-out loggers. A few fir seedlings were coming up now as high as the pheasants' heads, but they were almost crowded out by the faster-growing thickets of maple, alder, blackberry, wild currant, buckthorn, elderberry, and dogwood. These the pheasants noted with satisfaction, for they were much like the thickets they had known in their old homeland as places to find fruits and nuts and seed pods, and anything that meant food was to be remembered.

Three inborn needs governed their whole lives— the need for food, the need to stay alive and free, the need to have mates and young. For the hens in their first days of motherhood, the young would come first, but the War Lord lived by all three at once. Each day he had to separate *Do* from *Do Not* by the memory of what he himself had done in the past, but he was also guided by an unfathomable race memory that was his from birth, the gift of ancient pheasant ancestors, revealed to him by a complexity of sense organs in nerve, muscle, and tissue, an inherited pattern to which his life was woven. The pattern was as certain an inheritance as the very shape and color of his feathers, and the pattern—like his plumage—needed constant care to be kept bright. Any bird that failed in such preening seldom lived long enough to pass on its carelessness and stupidity to a new generation, and that was part of another pattern—nature's pattern for survival of the fittest.

The War Lord was well qualified to pass on pheasant lineage. Now, as surely as if he were on familiar

34

ground, he led his band of three to roost beneath a thick-branched evergreen. There First Mate and Number Two Hen and Little Three all slept confidently beside him, undisturbed by any feeling of rivalry, any hint of the coming need to begin seeking a nest, each one apart.

The War Lord was vaguely aware of the returning springtime cycle, but in this strange land the need to claim his territory had to come before he could go on to take his mates. Only when he was sure the land was his, with no rival cock near enough to crow defying challenge, could he feel the urge to begin his courtship. He did not know a conscious need to be secure in his homestake site before he could take a mate. The exigencies of weighing the worth of one good thing against another to choose which came first were not among the many problems life demanded of pheasant-kind. Problems he had in plenty, but the time of choosing a mate was not one of them.

For the War Lord, as for all wild things, large or small, fierce or gentle, the time of mating came with the pattern to which his life was woven. The signal to begin a new design could not be recognized until all the necessary threads were in place. He would know when the time was right for his courtship to begin. His own body would announce the signal, for

the glands and organs that had shrunk to functionless quiescence during the fall and winter would then come surging back to springtime's pulsating demand for life.

As yet, he knew only the faintest ripple of the coming change, and it made small impact on his senses against the overpowering need to beware of all the unknown dangers of this new terrain. Even the need for sleep did not free him from sentry duty, and he and the hens beside him only half slept.

4

The pheasants fed together in the early morning, coursing down the slope to the water's edge, drinking their fill and returning to the stump-filled clearing to feed again. Now the cock spied a huddle of beetles under a maple leaf and invited the hens to share them with indulgent, husbandly churking. They came obediently, but as he wandered on ahead, they began to look about on their own, each one drawn by some different object that was of familiar use—dusting hollow, lookout post, brambly hideaway where four-foot predators could not follow.

They saw no such prowlers, for the glen had been well hunted by nearby settlers who needed to protect their chickens from night raiders—and by others who hunted for food or pleasure. But the pheasants could learn of their safety only by living each day and night through on wary guard, and the weeks passed one by one without alarm, as March turned to April.

On a certain night in mid-April the War Lord felt an odd uneasiness come over him as he tried to settle in the roosting hollow. It was more than just discomfort from the rain-soaked earth beneath him, for in the past days he had become used to steady downpour and dampness. He thought he saw, he thought he heard warning of danger, but he looked again and saw nothing, heard no alien sound. He squirmed uneasily. Ground roost such as this was pheasant custom, and his feathers were usually insulation enough against damp and chill. Only in flight from enemies that came on foot did the pattern require him to seek escape in treetop roost. The threefold law of survival was a firm part of his heritage: Fly high from danger that walks. . . . Slink from danger that flies. . . . But if you have not yet been seen, remain motionless, for that which does not move does not catch the hunter's eye.

The War Lord knew the law. He knew also the age-old pheasant strategy of taking to wing with loud and jarring rattling of quills and pinions. Why he did so, he did not know, but he had learned that when he drummed out that rattling fusillade, a hawk might delay its plunging attack or a wildcat wait just long enough before breaking from crouching threat so that treetop roost might be gained in safety. Anything that had once meant the difference between life and death he remembered—and tried again.

There was no reason now to fly or slink. No enemy he could see. Still, he eyed the thick shelter of the fir branches uneasily.

The hens, well fed and drowsy, showed no signs of mistrust, but snuggled together in sisterly harmony, ruffling their feathers over their beaks for warmth. The War Lord let his head sink down between his shoulders also, and sleep took over all but that sixth sense that never quite submerged.

Suddenly he started up, then froze to instant immobility at the first almost inaudible rustle of nameless feather against feather, spread wing against air current. The hens, buried in their feather pillowing, did not even stir at this faintest of faint sounds. Warily, the cock began turning his head for a better view, moving so slowly that only sharp eyes already watching his hunched figure would have detected the movement. But eyes were watching—the incredibly sharp eyes of a great horned owl. On wings silenced by soft feather-edging of silken down, it swooped under the branches, spread talons seeking the outermost of those four huddled shapes, and on the cock's other side Little Three came wide awake, stretching herself to instant snake-slither beneath the bending grasses. Number Two Hen was not so quickly roused, and it was she who had the outside post. The spread talons hooked

41

into her flesh with killing grip, and her first startled squawk was her last.

The War Lord thundered up right in the owl's face with wing whir and war cry, but the owl was not startled into dropping its prey. It had long since learned about wing-whir trickery from hunting ruffed grouse, and it did not let such noise delay its death plunge. The talons closed firmly, and the owl was up and away, caught only momentarily off balance by the dangling tail plumes that were far longer than those of any other bird it had ever captured. Once the off-balance wing was set right again, the owl did not give the long barred tail a second glance. Food was food. Feathers were just something to be plucked out and tossed away or else rolled into tidy pellets by his stomach juices and spit out along with indigestible bones.

The War Lord kept tensely alert, following whatever traces of the owl's flight his senses could provide. Here amid thick-needled branches, yet not too close to the trunk where he would be in reach of some tree-climbing foe, he was fairly safe, and beside him First Mate was safe also, for she had followed his take-off without hesitation. Number Two Hen was gone, irretrievably, as they both knew. They had seen too many owls, too many swooping hawks seize chicks or flock mates not to know that she would never return. But where was Little Three?

Now from the ground below came a rustling that meant the stealthy squirming of a furry body pressed close to earth on hunting foray. Some four-foot prowler was following the owl's trail, ready to capture whatever creature might be still trembling from narrow escape— too frightened or too relieved to watch for a second enemy.

Was Little Three its target?

"K-k-k-kruk!" called the War Lord in guttural warning, but the low-pitched sound had just begun to roll when Little Three's own voice jetted explosive alarm, and she came sailing up to the fir branch to join the others.

On the ground below, the black-masked figure of a raccoon came out into a patch of moonlight, its night-keen eyes following the hen to her safe perch. Now it lifted its head in the long-drawn-out wavering call that the pheasants would have taken for owl cry if they had not seen it coming from a furry creature with big ringed tail and black mask, for there are no raccoons in China—nor anywhere else except the Americas, unless men have transplanted them. But both cock and hens knew other furry prowlers who counted pheasants as fair prey, and now they added this new

43

one to a long list of enemies.

Quivering, Little Three edged closer to the others on the high roost. Like all pheasants, she had known from birth the law of survival, but now she had learned it anew with her own life as reward: Slink from an enemy that flies; fly from the enemy that creeps afoot.

Perhaps if the War Lord had been on familiar ground, or if sunny days had dried out the old nesting hollow, the high treetop roost would have remained escape perch only. But he was in new terrain, alert to adapt old ways to new needs, and the rains continued. For the next few nights, he led the hens to a lofty sleeping perch, and he would continue to do so often in Oregon's frequent drizzles and downpours that left the ground hollows uncomfortably damp. For his children and their children, the habit would become imitative family custom. But for the War Lord it was survival's choice—part instinct, part cunning.

5

Within the week the cold and damp gave way to a
red-splashed sunset that promised a clear and star-
bright night and blue skies on the morrow. And the
promise was kept. The stars were still bright when
the first faint dawn streaks appeared. Cock robins began to sing even before daybreak, chiding the tardy
sunrise with rousing carol that boasted proof of their
own readiness for another spring of courting and
nesting and rearing speckled-front, gaping-mouthed
young. The robin's morning song had scarce begun
when the War Lord heard the buzzy love-trill of the
towhee, another early riser that did not wait for morning's full light. Only half heard against towhee trill
and robin carol came the soft and pleading whistle of
a white-crowned sparrow, a begging serenader, not a
boaster who seemed ready to demand his lover's rights.
Now a song sparrow joined in the medley with three-
note ripple and a trill, and the War Lord was wide
awake, ready for action.

He was off the roosting bough with a ruffle of

feathers, a stretching of each night-bound muscle and tendon, and making his way to that certain spot that had already become his favorite lookout post, the first place where he came each morning to crow, renewed claim to all the land within good echo of his battle cry. With arching throat and half-lifted wings, he sounded the challenge—two clarion trumpet notes and a drum-beat ruffle of wings for emphasis.

He waited, listening. Any answer near at hand would mean that a rival defied his claim to the land and freehold rights. For a moment he thought he heard that answer, but only faintly and at too great a distance to be serious challenge. Still, he had to be sure, and so he went on a few steps to repeat the trumpet-and-drumbeat declaration, keeping carefully to the line he had already marked as the farthest uphill limit of his domain.

The line was only a rutted scar of bared earth left where an ox team had dragged log after log across the rise to the water's edge for floating downriver to a sawmill. The stream was no longer deep enough for logging—had not been since a rancher named Kentucky Hallowell had dammed it up above to make a watering place for his brood mares and prized stallions, brought from his namesake state on western fortune-hunter's venture. The logger, who had neglected to make sure of his water rights before he bought his land, sold out to another greenhorn who wouldn't think to ask—a Southerner named Clay Sharon, come West like so many other old soldiers of the Confederacy in a last hope of finding a place where it was neither North nor South but only America. If Clay's son Randolph had lived, they might have given Tuck Hallowell a fight for the water, but young Randy and his wife Anne had both been taken off by the black croup in the terrible blizzard year of 1880, leaving only old Clay and his wife Melissa and the ten-year-old grandson Jed. Now, with only the boy to help him, there was no thought of logging, no need for a deeper river, since the potatoes and young plum orchard he planted got all the water they needed from the light but frequent rains. Old Clay and the boy came to the glen sometimes for firewood to use or to sell, but there was no longer the daily crossing of plodding oxen and heavy logs, and so the old ruts had become only a blurring trace by the time the War Lord chose them for a boundary line, the place on which he stood to declare ownership with trumpet-and-drumbeat clarion.

Once again he sent his call ringing down the glen, and this time he was sure he heard no answer. The land was his, the time was spring, and he could claim his brides.

He caught First Mate's watching eyes and began parading for her in the ancestral love dance he had never had to learn but knew from nature's own compulsion, pecking the hard ground before her with sharp beak, stamping stoutly with spurred feet to make sure that she understood that the display was for her alone. Now, with head downbent in graceful arc, he ruffled wing and flank feathers outward toward her, all flowing to one side and separating feather from feather, so that he must have seemed to grow twice size before her very eyes, and sending his barred tail feathers pluming out behind him in iridescent amber rainbow.

Thus he took First Mate to wife with regal assurance, and later he claimed skittish Little Three. She was a yearling, finding herself the first time a coquette to be conquered, and she kept moving away from him as if uncertain of her role—or not yet ready for it. When she stepped away, the War Lord stepped after her—ran after her, darting toward her with half-furled feathers, feinting to the right, to the left, scuttling ahead of her to cut off retreat, driving her at last to a corner from which there was no escape and he could complete the ritual dance pattern with full assurance that each step, each boldly spread feather would be watched in wonder—and in final capitulation.

Daily thereafter he repeated the ceremony, with

each hen in turn as watching admirer in accordance with pheasant custom. From time to time he walked alone with each hen in courtship twosome now, and he stood guard while each one chose her nesting site, and soon both of his mates were ready to begin laying. In each nest the olive-buff eggs grew in number, but there would be no brooding till the accepted number for pheasant hatch would be complete—usually ten to twelve.

There were just three eggs in Little Three's nest when a Beechey's ground squirrel discovered it, and he cracked one shell greedily, leaving jagged, tooth-torn rim, and sucking up the contents in such haste that a telltale yellow trickle spilled down his chin. Just as a second yellow trickle followed the first, the War Lord returned from his usual cruising survey and caught the culprit in the very act of reaching for a third helping. Before the little paws could close around the shell, the War Lord was launching to attack and the squirrel dropped the egg and fled, reaching the safety of his burrow just seconds before the hooked beak would have slashed into gray fur. Now Little Three came back to find disaster, and the War Lord stayed beside her, keeping up a low-voiced churking and a wary lookout.

If incubation had been well along, with hatching

day near, Little Three would no doubt have covered the remaining egg instantly, for the demands of motherhood take precedence over all else. But now at this early date the eggs were just eggs, easily replaced, with brooding not even begun. So she chose to make a new nest elsewhere and start over, leaving the untouched egg beside the broken shells. Soon the new nest also held three eggs, then four, then five—and she continued the laying for the accustomed two-week span.

Now incubation would keep her on the nest a good three weeks more, for hatching does not usually begin till the twenty-second day after the last egg is laid. During this time the War Lord would keep constant guard, with no more courting dances to offer distraction from duties. His low-voiced *k-k-k* of caution advised Little Three and First Mate of every egg-hunting ground squirrel or snake, crow, jay, or magpie that came within his boundaries by day; every skunk, raccoon, weasel, or barnyard cat that might come by night. If the hens were on the nests where they belonged, it was a warning to lie motionless, letting their leaf-matching colors keep them unseen, or to slink well away from the eggs before showing themselves for decoy target. If they were feeding, his call warned them not to return to the nest till the raider had passed. Now in these days the hens had no scent that prowlers who followed their noses might detect, and if they could remain motionless, those who hunted by eye would also have no clue. Still, now and then some egg-hunter might come dangerously close, and the cock was always ready to fly up with noisy clatter and tempting show that few predators could resist.

Luckily, no raider found the two nests—or at least did not find them unguarded. Even the crows and jays did not dare steal eggs when this newcomer with fierce cry and fiercer beak was watching. The owl that had taken Number Two Hen had been killed the next day by young Jed Sharon, who dispatched other egg-eating creatures without even knowing that he did the pheasants a service, for he had not yet learned of their presence.

The pheasants were unaware of Jed also, and the War Lord took to himself full credit for continued safety. He cruised his domain three or four times each day, keeping wary eye on every corner in the meandering circle marked by a half-mile radius from the fir tree that had been first night roost. If he had found himself in the midst of enemies or with scanty food supply or had lost his mates to some predator, he would never have been content to stay in such small area. Indeed, other pheasants released on the other side of the butte had been set upon by barnyard cats left to forage for their own food, and the mateless cocks had wandered to amazing distances, calling, calling day after day without answer from any hen of their own kind.

One lonely cock had traveled full fifty miles in the first two months, and when at last he could stand it no longer without a mate, he swaggered into a chicken-yard and convinced the astonished rooster to run squawking for the woods and leave the hens to be entranced by strange courtship prancing. The courting was not completely strange, for barnyard birds are descended from the red jungle fowl of India, a not too distant pheasant cousin. They are too distantly re-lated, however, to produce fertile chicks. And the hens were too far away from jungle ancestry to will-ingly follow the cock to the fields. When they turned down his invitation to wander, he went on alone, still feeling that the inherited pattern of his life had not been fulfilled, and eventually tried his charms in other chickenyards.

Any friends of John and Owen Denny put up with such visitors, willingly allowing the birds—cocks or hens—to feed in peace. But that fifty-mile rover came one day into a henyard where the Dennys and their China birds were unknown. The rooster was a scrappy Rhode Island Red, big enough to give the invader spur for spur—for a few minutes. When the outraged farmwife saw the battle, she reached for a gun and took care of the intruder with one shot. She wrung the neck with the white torque ring, plunged the bright-feathered body into scalding water for easy plucking and cooked the cock for supper, scarcely noticing that it was of a kind never before seen. But when the bird was browned in the rich drippings from her home-cured bacon and simmered under cover till tender—and with a dollop of thick cream added at the last minute to flavor the gravy—the meat had such a delicious taste that she wished she'd taken a better look and could recognize the bird if she ever saw another.

The War Lord was forced to no such philandering misadventure. Guarding his two mates was challenge enough. The hens showed every sign of being grateful for his care and left their nest to feed only when he was near, obeying his warning command to slink away or freeze in invisible camouflage, instantly and without question. Nevertheless, if the cock were not near when danger threatened, they could choose the proper strategy themselves. Soon the chicks would be hatching, and then the hens would have to rely even more on their own wisdom, for young birds have to roam or they will never learn the ways of their world, and the cock could not keep track of both broods at once.

6

The War Lord was busy fighting a bull snake near Little Three's belated nest at the precise moment when the first egg began to crack open in First Mate's brood. Unaware that his eldest son was chipping through the shell with energetic blows from the egg-tooth on the tiny beak, the big cock concentrated on his slippery foe, dancing around the cornered snake with darting feint and stab. The snake would have swallowed egg or hatchling or both with hungry dispatch, for it, too, lived by a pattern, with the need for food the drive that made it a relentless hunter and the War Lord's foe. When the cock finally made the kill, the snake was no longer foe, but food, and he regarded it with no more ill-will than he would have found for tarweed or dandelion.

Meanwhile, other eggs in First Mate's nest were beginning to show faint cracking, and Eldest Brother had his pearl-tint shell chipped a good two-thirds around. Now as he struggled out, a damp and wriggling blob, the top fell back as if on sturdy hinge, clinging to his tailless behind, and he suddenly gave up the struggle to be rid of it, flopping into awkward half-squat sprawl. First Mate called to him with the low, sweet chirpings she would use only in the first hours of motherhood, a tender and coaxing cradle song, and once more he tried to be rid of the shell and find his feet.

Soon other chicks were needing her encouragement, too, for all the eggs had been brooded the same length of time and all would hatch this day. By late afternoon there were ten bright-eyed mites tottering about on wobbly pink legs that seemed absurdly long, and the fast-drying birthdown was beginning to fluff out in a buff and brown dappling that looked like a pattern traced by sunlight falling through leafy branches.

First Mate rose to her feet, shaking her feathers for quick preening, calling her chicks to follow. Instinct told her to leave the nest with its odorous egg shells as quickly as possible, for both she and the chicks were without scent to attract predators and the protection would be useless so long as she stayed near those tell-tale shells.

Down the glen she went, with the chicks bobbing and peeping behind her, and at last she came to an inviting nook. Here under a tangle of bracken and blackberry vines she settled down, somehow managing to coax and nudge all ten chicks under her ruffled feathers for warmth and a good night's rest. By first dawn light they were awake and ready to come squirming out again, each one bursting with curiosity, energy, and insatiable appetite. Only by eating all day every day could they fuel their bodies for the rapid growth that would take them from hatchling to adult in one brief season, and they had been born knowing how to catch their own food. Without delay they began snapping at the first fly to come buzzing within reach, the first bug and beetle to crawl into view, for insects would be their instinctive choice of menu these first weeks.

But although instinct told them much of pheasant pattern, there were still things they needed to be taught. According to custom, First Mate was in full charge of this schooling and did not expect the War Lord's help, beyond his usual danger watch. First of all, the chicks needed to learn obedience, unfaltering response to their mother's voice, and though response was instinctive, it needed to be reinforced with continual daily practice. Each change of her voice had different meaning, and the gentle cluck that simply meant "Come along—don't dawdle" was not so sharp as the call to come quickly and feast on squirming caterpillars before they vanished. If she took off suddenly in silent flight, they learned to crouch instantly right where they were. But if her flight was accompanied by a rattling *chuck-chuck-chuck-it* of full alarm, they were to scurry for the nearest thicket or bramble patch, for they had been seen by some foe and the quick-freeze could not save them. In these first days before the chicks learned to fly, the hen followed up her rattling take-off with a quick return to the ground and a well-feigned mimicry of broken wing and limping gait that would make the prowler forget the chicks in hopes of her plumper reward. The moment he came too near, she would take to wing again, disappearing into the thickets, and would not return to the chicks until the hunter had gone away, seeking easier game elsewhere.

The chicks would be where she'd left them, as limp as so many dead leaves, but at her rally call they would come popping out of hiding, ready to follow wherever she led. Some came more quickly than others, for in any brood there seem to be a few dilly-dally loiterers. But all kept up a squeaky *peep-peep* as they toddled after her, as if answering a continual roll call. Any dawdler that suddenly found itself alone, cut off from view of the others by bush or boulder, would explode into screeching, high-pitched alarm until First

Mate's familiar clucking guided it back to the family parade.

Little Three's brood hatched now, also, and the damp and squirming blobs struggled from their shells and turned into fluffy toddlers in dappled down under her watchful gaze. This was her first brood, and she had no memory of another hatching except her own, yet she guided them away from the broken shells to a new nesting place as cautiously as First Mate had done. But on this night a misty, soak-through-everything drizzle made complete drying difficult, and a sudden sweep of cold north wind made matters worse. The rain froze as it fell, coating everything it touched in glistening silver-ice prison. Twigs, grass blades, the first buds on the wild rose—all were sheathed in glittering glassy casement. The chicks, too, were pelted by the freezing drops, and Little Three strove frantically to get them all under her body, clucking and ruffling despairingly as one squirmed out behind her as soon as she nudged another into place, and their peeping cries added to her distress.

Luckily, few prowlers were out in such weather, but the War Lord thought he saw the black shadow of a skunk slinking through the bushes and held himself at motionless alert. He kept watcher's pose so long that his drooping tail plumes were soon frozen fast by their icy coating. If he had had to take off suddenly now as a decoy, his entire tail would have been left behind, but the skunk went back to its den to wait out the storm. Now at last the War Lord could begin to twist himself free, patiently, carefully, but the ice had thickened with the run-off of water from the bent branches above him, and would not yield. It was a temptation just to jerk and be done with it, but the cock waited, and just before dawn the north wind suddenly died down and the sun rose in a cloudless sky. For a few moments the hill was a shining wonderland of translucent silver overlay on branch, buds, and grass—the Willamette Valley's famous "Silver Thaw." Then the silver icing melted beneath the sun's touch, and the cock twisted free with only disarray to mark his imprisonment.

But Little Three rose to find the chicks beneath her chilled and lifeless. As she stared, grief-stricken, one small eye blinked open, one little head moved—then another—and another. But that was all. Only three were still alive. Two little sisters and a spunky brother. But three were enough to fulfill her role of motherhood—even one chick would have roused all her instincts. And now instinct commanded her to put aside her first grief for the lost chicks and give all her strength to the living. It was the only possible rule for creatures that lived always in the presence of death, the only sensible way. But Little Three had no thought of being sensible; she was just the way she was. Three chicks needed her care, and she would give them all she had to give.

7

The chicks' two-week birthday was marked by sprouting armor of quills for back and flank feathers, and the downy softness was lost forever. They were eating buds and grass tops now, as well as the insects that had yielded their first protein-rich fare, but they would never lose their appetite for the aphids, beetles, spiders, grasshoppers, ants, and locusts that had satisfied first hunger.

Occasionally now the War Lord would join either First Mate or Little Three on daily promenade, but he seldom stayed long with either band, and the chicks paid him little attention.

By five weeks the poults were full feathered, but they immediately began moulting this juvenal plumage and the feathers that grew in replacement were of adult pattern. At seven weeks the young cockerels were beginning to show a hint of spurs on sturdy legs, and the first touches of masculine coloring set them off plainly from their sisters. Now and then they would try a feeble imitation of the War Lord's trumpet-and-

61

drumbeat challenge, and they were all capable of quick gliding flight.

It was important now that the mothers lead their broods farther afield to learn the ways of a wider world, and the War Lord gave up his first close guard. There was nothing of carelessness or laziness or shirking of duty in this relaxing of watchfulness. It was part of the pattern that would in time lead each cockerel to go out beyond his father's boundaries and seek mate and territory for himself.

In addition, there was also the inescapable fact that three full-grown pheasants and thirteen growing poults needed an amazing amount of food, and the glen's larder did not always suffice now. The wandering forays of First Mate and Little Three had already found the potato field that Clay Sharon had planted and also his new orchard of young plum trees not yet in fruit. On the other side of the glen they had come to the oatfield that Kentucky Hallowell was raising for his horses, but they had not ventured beyond the outer edges of either field and were sure that no human had seen them.

Of the two broods, it was Little Three's that seemed to give their mother the most trouble. Three should certainly have been easier to care for than ten, but she had gotten off to a bad start with discipline and now the more she clucked at them, the more they seemed to wander off on their own. She was always having to chase after them, coax them away from some danger zone, and as a result she lived in a continual state of hastily abandoned meals and half-finished naps.

Hunger nagged at her now as she led her trio out of the glen toward the orchard. She had watched yesterday while a man with a mule plowed up all the land between the young trees, turning under the weeds that had been choking them, and afterwards she had found the opened furrows good hunting for all sorts of grubs and insects. For once the chicks were on good behavior, coming along obediently in her wake, blending from one safe cover patch to the next, with cautious survey in between, as she had taught them. Now that the weeds were plowed under, the orchard did not give them much protection, for the young trees scarcely cast a shadow, but the humped rows of brown earth clods were of almost the same shape and coloring as the brown-feathered birds, and Little Three was not unduly disturbed by crossing into the clearing.

She proceeded slowly, as she always did, looking to the right, looking to the left, before walking on. Her sharp eyes were watching for the slightest movement on the ground or in the air that might be warning of danger. Her ears registered each sound. But for her as for other hunters, that which made no sound or movement was likely to go unnoticed. She did not see a silent, motionless shadow high up on a fir branch, no more obtrusive than a misshapen cone among a cluster of needles.

That shadow, however, was made by the blue-gray and russet plumage of a sharp-shinned hawk, and his gleaming, hungry eyes had been aware of the pheasants from the moment they stepped into the clearing. He had watched these strange, chickenlike birds before, but never with the odds so much in favor of successful hunting. He was small, compared to other hawks, and relied on the swiftness of surprise attack from hidden perch—or on his uncanny talent for getting through tangled brush by reason of short, rounded wings and a long tail that gave instant change-of-direction. The trouble was that just now his skill was somewhat lessened by a lame wing, barely healed from a gunshot wound inflicted by Jed Sharon when the sharpshin had tried to raid the family's chickenyard. Till the wing was fully healed, he would have to forego his usual brush-tangle chasing and rely only on surprise attack. So now these strange chicks feeding in the open seemed to be there just for his pleasure. The hen, of course, was too big for his twelve-inch length to handle, but the chicks would be just right. He put all thoughts of the hen aside and concentrated on the chicks, watching each hop-skip movement as they stopped eating and began leaping from furrow to furrow.

The little cock was in the lead, as usual, well pleased with his new game. Every jump took him farther from his mother and closer to the big fir, and the two sisters came right behind him. Little Three looked up, seeing the widening distance, the careless unconcern, and clucked stern reminder. At that moment the gray blur plunged downward, hooked talons arching for the death grip.

The hen's cluck turned to a wild cry, and the chicks flattened into the furrows, fear frozen. Little Three leaped to meet the plunging death mid-air, wings flared wide, hooked beak ready for raking slash, not needing to be told that the leap left her own soft breast defenseless against those seeking talons, needing still less to be told that it was mother-right to give her life for her chicks, if that was the price now demanded.

The hawk, startled by the unexpected leap—by the width of those flared wings thrust suddenly between him and his intended prey—reacted with involuntary sideslip, and the lame wing tossed him into head-over-tail somersault. Before he could right himself, the hen's command had sent the chicks scuttling for the blackberry thicket, and the strange birds were as lost to the sharpshin as if never a pheasant had ever left China.

Now the cock came hurtling down the ridge, racing to battle at the sound of his mate's alarm cry. Three times the sharpshin's length, he seemed formidable adversary indeed, and the hawk did not wait to test his challenge. Open warfare with the odds against him was not the means by which he had learned survival, and now with one reconnoitering dip and dive he was off to seek another hunting ground. Past experience had taught him that he would find no unwary prize to capture while any bird sounded alarm as vociferous as the cock's *ky-urking* battle cry. Every sparrow in the glen, every fieldmouse, everything in fur and feathers that crept or crawled or flew could understand that message of danger.

Without a backward glance, the sharpshin climbed skyward, and three crows in the next field, seeing their rival chick-snatcher in full retreat, took up the chase with taunting croaks. The War Lord watched them all out of sight, garnet eyes still alert for any hint that either hawk or crows might turn back for a sneak attack. But at last he was satisfied that they had gone and churked at Little Three and the crouching chicks with reassuring tone.

But the hen waited still longer to call her trio to come from their hiding places. The plunging shadow of rounded wings and long tail that mark the accipiter hawks was an image that neither she nor the chicks would ever forget.

PART II

THE BOY AND THE GUN

1

For a few days after the battle with the hawk, all of the pheasants stayed away from the plowed land of the young orchard. But the scanty larder of the well-gleaned glen could no longer satisfy so many appetites, especially for the chicks, whose rapid growth demanded almost their own weight in bugs, buds, and beetles each day. Hunger would not let them hide, and they began foraging farther and farther afield, venturing closer and closer to the Sharon woodlot and the Sharon barnyard where the sharp-shinned hawk had learned its first lesson about a boy and a gun—a lesson that the pheasants did not even know awaited them.

The woodlot was closer to the glen and therefore seemed safer haven, although old Clay and his grandson Jed had been working there of late, chopping cord after cord of wood in expectation of hauling it down to the Willamette and selling it to the river steamers. The ring of sharp ax biting into live wood, the clatter of rolling logs as the boy stumbled and dropped another armload made a warning racket that kept the pheasants at safe distance. Small need to fear so noisy a foe, ran the wisdom of wildlife instinct. Later, when boy and man had gone and the woodlot was quiet again, the growing stacks of wood had at first seemed fearsome simply because they were strange, but in time the rectangular hulks became familiar and lost their fearsomeness, seeming no more foreign than the trees from which they had been hewn.

Today, neither boy nor man had come to the woodlot, having insistent chores elsewhere, and the War Lord, with Little Three and her brood coming ragtag at his heels, found that the whole clearing was their well-spread table. Even the goldfinches and sparrows had not come here to glean while the woodchoppers were about their racket and clatter, and the seed pods bulged full on ripening stalk and stem. Cock, hen and eager gangling chicks—halfgrown pullets and cockerel now, and babes no longer—bent to their feasting. A flock of goldfinches came to join them, sweeping into the clearing with dip-and-glide flight and a chorus of lisping twitters, but the pheasants scarcely glanced up. There was enough for all.

Then without any warning the War Lord had heard, the little yellow birds with the black caps were off and away, and he lifted his head for wary survey. What had they seen that he had missed?

He did not have to ask the question twice. He could see the enemy for himself now. It was the boy—only the boy, and the man was not with him this time. And the boy was not coming with noisy and careless tell-the-world stomping, as he usually did. He came with only the faintest of telltale rustle, stepping carefully, and pausing to hold up one hand for eyeshade as he searched the clearing from side to side. Now he stretched up on tiptoe, scanning the surrounding tree-top fringe of evergreens. Now he bent low, searching behind stump and weed patch.

Searching for what?

With warning shiver, the War Lord knew the answer. Somehow, although the boy had given no sign or signal as he worked at the wood stack, somehow he had seen the pheasants and come back to hunt for them. Every action bespoke the hunter. The stealthy approach. The careful searching. Patience instead of racket-clatter haste to get a job done and get out. Oh, yes, this was a hunter. No matter that he came on two legs instead of four—the way of the hunter was always the same and to the wary it was always fair warning.

Cautiously, the War Lord turned his head towards the left where Little Three had been feeding a moment before, and he saw that she, too, had been alerted by the goldfinches' sudden departure and now had the boy in view. He was in mid-clearing now; he gave a full-span circling look, then eased down on a stump with slow and careful settling. He had been carrying some sort of odd-shaped stick, and now he let it rest full length across his knees so that he had both hands free to use for shaded search to right and left. If the War Lord had ever seen a gun before, he would have taken to instant snake-slither escape then and there, without a half breath of delay. But he had not seen a gun before, nor heard gunfire explosion. In the old homeland, the men who came to his fields and glens were poor farm folk and had only net and snare or homemade trap. These he had learned to avoid— though not always, or he would not now be here in this new land that was still not quite home.

But although he had not learned everything about avoiding these human two-legged hunters, he had learned much, and now the War Lord called on his store of wisdom to direct his strategy. As always, what had been successful tactic before would be tried again. And what was most successful, so far as men were concerned, was keeping well out of reach. The birds that stayed well away from the place where a man sat waiting were not the ones caught in the flung net. The birds that stayed well away from the places where men walked were not the ones caught in the tightening loop.

74

It was especially wise to stay away from two-legged hunters who sat as this one did now, with that certain searching look in his eyes. The hunter's look always betrayed him. The War Lord had seen it in the big yellow eyes of a slinking wildcat, in the glittering lidless eyes of a snake, in the fierce red-eyed glare of a goshawk or its smaller sharp-shinned cousin, in the slanted eyes of the men of his old homeland. Now he saw the same look in the wide blue eyes of freckle-faced Jed Sharon.

If the cock had been alone and caught in this predicament, he would have followed the usual escape pattern that had worked so often when he had spied the hunter before he himself had been discovered. Without moving the grasstops to betraying rustle he could sink to a ground-hugging crouch and melt away into the underbrush, seeming more snakelike than avian in his flowing movement. But he was not alone. Little Three and her three poults were there also, and experience had taught him that the chances for all of them to slip away unseen were not good, unless the watching eye of the hunter could be led astray by some distraction from another quarter.

Instinct had provided the War Lord with just such distracting tactic, and without debate or delay he put it to action. One zigzag slither to the left—one more—

With rousing *k-k-kuk* of defiance for the hunter and warning to hen and poults, he exploded into the air on powerful spreadwing sweep and quill-rattling tattoo, sounding again his battlecry. Out of the corner of his wide-circle gaze, he caught a glimpse of the boy in half-caught stumble—the leap of surprise halted midair by a fumbling effort to retrieve his gun and bring it to shoulder for steady aim. The movement caught thus by the pheasant's eye was blurred but clear enough for warning, if he had known the meaning of a gun lifted for sighting.

It was an old gun, and far from accurate, but the boy had become used to its tricks through much practice, and his finger found the trigger curve almost of itself, without conscious direction, and the roar of its discharge shook the air, launching the bullet on the same high curve set by the War Lord's wings.

With a heaving thrust of straining muscles, the big bird flung himself forward into the sheltering branches of a great fir, seeing now for the first time that Little Three had followed him in midair leap, adding her own delaying strategy that would give her young ones time to reach safe hiding place. She had leaped from the weed patch just a breath gasp behind him, and was close behind him now as he reached for the fir bough with hooked talon and flailing wing.

But she was not close enough.

The bullet meant for the War Lord found Little Three instead and the watching cock saw her caught motionless by the impact in lightning-flash brevity before she crumpled in a shower of feathers and went tumbling to the ground in the awkwardness of death.

The boy, standing there with eyes and mouth both wide in amazement at the killing of a bird he had not even seen amid his trancelike watching of the cock, did not even move forward at first to pick her up. But he did so, finally, and as he bent over her the War Lord slipped into the air on silent wings, keeping the trees between him and the hunter for safety's sake, knowing that he had been the prey the hunter sought—and would seek again, using this new death-that-comes-with-thunderclap.

On the ground below, safely out of the clearing in a well-tangled blackberry clump, the three young pheasants had seen only half of what had happened, for they had gone off pellmell in obedient scramble for cover at their mother's alarm signal. But they had heard the gunblast and turned in time to see her in deathfall. They had seen the cock take off on the silent wings of safety, and they knew that the enemy must still be at hand. Until the all-clear signal should come, they would not leave their hiding place nor make betraying sound or movement. That was a lesson that both instinct and their mother's sharp reminders had taught them well.

But never before had the all-clear signal been so long in coming. Never before had the waiting for her soft come-to-me clucking seemed so endless. They heard the boy tromping about, as if looking for something, and then at last even the sound of his clumsy footsteps faded away, and the restless little cockerel poked out a curious head.

Above him a pair of jays began sudden fusillade screaming at a huddled blob of feathers they had just discovered to be a screech owl in daylight siesta, and the startled cockerel ducked back into the thorny fortress with his sisters. They did not move again, even though the owl flew off in search of quieter quarters and the jays followed, taking their noisy rattlings with them.

The boy was gone, too. Listening, looking, listening again, the three trembling chicks were sure there was no enemy near, yet the familiar all-clear did not come. Their mother had given the command to wait —then nothing more.

They waited—and waited. And now in the quiet of approaching dusk they set up a plaintive, piping search cry, calling for their mother, hunting her down the grass-tunnel paths, with the two little sisters led as usual by the bolder cockerel.

"Pee-eep! Peep, peep, pee-eep!" the trio of voices rang out.

Their cries, begun in puzzled bewilderment at lack of maternal guidance, soon heightened to panic's shrill. Neither their mother nor the cock answered, and they wandered on, still calling, and at last the hit-and-miss search brought them stumbling into a flock of grasshoppers. The sight of this tasty meal was an answer to their hunger, if not to loneliness, and somehow in satisfying one need, the other seemed less sharply demanding.

Overhead the twilight shadows were deepening, and the new need for a roosting place set them on piping search cry again, asking for their mother to find them and lead them to safe shelter. Now the cockerel squirmed under a blackberry vine and onto a familiar path, the sisters after him, and all three discovered at the same moment that they had come out at one of Little Three's favorite roosting spots—a thick-grown spruce whose pungent, low-spreading branches had often given them night shelter. They hopped up into its covering as promptly as if their mother had been there to give command, and settled down with their usual play of pushing and shoving each other in rivalry

79

for the post next the trunk. The branch was familiar, but the chill brush of wind that came without their mother's sheltering body seemed frighteningly strange and first one and then the others lifted wide-open eyes to stare around, peeping plaintive protest. Then from nearby came the rustle of some night creature and the chicks hushed instantly and in a little while were fast asleep.

No nightmares troubled their slumber, no wakefulness. They had not yet developed that wary sixthsense for danger that was the War Lord's talisman, but it would come soon—sooner than if their mother had stayed at their side to let her wariness take full charge. The pattern of all pheasant growing was within them, a rightful heritage to claim as needed. Now they were scarcely half feathered, but in a few weeks—late September—full plumage would be theirs. At eleven weeks of age the cockerel would shed his stub tail for the adult's tail plume, although he would not attain full size and brilliance for another two months after that, and even then his spurs would be well short of the War Lord's gray and horny weapons.

Tonight they had missed their mother, but longheld grief was not part of the pattern. They had never known the blind and helpless babyhood that endangers songbird nestlings and the young of the big-bodied birds of prey when they are orphaned. These chicks had been able to run about and snap up flitting insects the moment their birthdown dried, and hunger would be all the guide they needed in this well-stocked glen. By November or December they would have been on their own, even if Little Three had not been killed. But she would have been able to teach them much of her own hard-won wisdom in those weeks, the wariness they would now have to gain on their own—or perish.

The question that Fate now asked, was this: Could chicks so young avoid hawks by day and owls by night; would they know the difference in grass rustle made by passing breeze and by a hungry cat?

The chicks themselves asked no questions. For them, all time was resolved into a Now, and since the only need of the moment was sleep, they slept soundly.

2

Far away, the War Lord sought sundown roost with the same singleness of need and purpose. He knew he was far from the home glen, for he had been driven by a fear beyond all measuring when the gunfire had burst upon him. He had never heard a gun fire before at close range, never before known what it meant to be target for such a weapon. This weapon was one against which neither heritage nor experience had given him the right defense tactics. The old law told him to fly high from danger that walks, but he and Little Three had flown from the walking boy and when the boy had lifted his arms, pointing upward, death had struck down his mate with terrifying noise.

He had seen her fall. Shielded by her body, he had made his getaway and the boy had not followed. He had made other terrifying noises, though, and so the War Lord had gone on and on until he could hear no further sound. His fear had been great, but not great enough to make him miss the meaning of the sound of gunfire or the shape of a gun. From now on the silhouette of a man with a gun would always hold different warning from the familiar man-shape, and the sound of gunfire would never again send him in high flight, an easy target.

In the morning he ate quickly, for he was restless away from the home glen. The need to defend his home was still strong within him, and so he started back on foot in a journey that began to seem inexplicably long. He had no way of comparing the swiftness of yesterday's fear flight with the slowness of today's patient plodding, with need always to stop, look, listen for danger. He kept on, expecting that over the next rise, around the next bramble patch, would be familiar territory.

The sun was high in the sky when he suddenly stepped around a hawthorn tree and came face to face with a pheasant hen. She saw him at the same moment and crouched submissively, giving him the welcome due a courting mate. He was surprised, but not unready to respond, and took another step into the clearing. All at once she sprang up with the who-goes-there challenge for a stranger and the cock gave stranger's questioning reply.

They were not exactly strangers, since they had been together in the bamboo courtyard on the *Isle of Bute* for seven long weeks. But for any mated hen, any cock except her own is a stranger and would never, never be welcomed, except by mistake, as this hen had done, thinking he was her mate. She had been waiting for her mate to begin courtship again, for she had recently lost the whole of her first hatching to raiding cats from nearby farms and was eager to start a new family. The War Lord did not understand her reason for withdrawal, but he had recognized her first invitation clearly and now he stepped forward in tentative dance step.

Suddenly from behind him came a whistling shriek of challenge, and he tried to whirl about-face in time to meet the hurtling attack of the hen's rightful mate. Caught off balance and unwarned, he barely managed to dodge the first beak thrust, but now the advantage of surprise was lost to his assailant, and the fight was even. Interloper the War Lord might be, but there was no step in the pattern to call for apology and withdrawal. He could fight and win or fight and lose, but he had to fight.

The two contenders drew themselves up to full height, feathers ruffled to full limit, and now came rushing together in frenzy. Hooked beak, flailing wing, and ready spurs were all the weapons they had, and all they needed. Slash! Rake! Slash! Strike!

The War Lord felt the red blood spurt across his

white torque collar, felt a second jagged blow from a driving beak and managed to twist aside just enough to escape the throat-slitting slash that would have ended everything. He gasped in renewed breath, sprang back to the battle, now tasting enemy blood on his own beak, drew back to gather momentum for another charge. The challenger was drawing up in the same maddening pose when suddenly a blue-gray shadow plunged downward—a shadow armed with the killer's talons of a Cooper's hawk, the sharp-shin's twice-size kin.

The War Lord tried to halt his leap midair, saw the hawk turn belly-over, felt the raking slash on his wings, then saw the hawk swerve to meet lunging attack from the rival cock. The War Lord, weakened as he was by the double onslaught, still rallied strength enough to fling himself beneath the hawthorn branches and crumpled there in a bloody heap.

He did not look up to see the hawk take wing with long-tailed prize dangling in its talons, and the hawk did not look down to seek the bird it had missed. One at a time was its rule. It killed to eat, not to strike terror, but its hunger was such that terror rode always in its wake. It did not usually attack two cocks at once —especially two this size—but it had seen the battle and the blood and knew that the birds were weakening.

Its only mistake was in judging that they had drawn aside in defeat, not to spring back to renewed battle, and that neither bird would be able to stop its lunge.

Daylight faded to dusk, and darkness was followed at last by graying dawn, and still the War Lord did not move. His very weakness was his strength, for his inability to struggle out from the thorn branches kept his blood clotted over his wounds so that there was no further loss, and his body began to heal. He had been eating well for weeks and had reserves to call on now in this time of need and did not feel undue hunger. A few grass tips still touched with dew quenched his thirst and then he slept again.

When he wakened the next day, he saw that the strange hen had slept beside him and was now waiting for him to take command. He knew then that the other cock would not return, for if her first mate still lived, the hen would have remained with him, not the newcomer. Now she was accepting the victor, as pheasant custom and her own need for a mate required.

The War Lord's wisdom—that blending of instinct and experience that guided his every move—now urged him to leave this place of battle, for where a hawk has killed once, it would come to kill again. Also, he felt instinctive desire to find his own terrain where First Mate and her chicks and the orphans of

Little Three were still in need of his care. His wounds were healed. He was once more a leader.

"K-k-k," he commanded the hen, getting to his feet. He felt the sudden sharp reminder of his hunger, but he could eat as he traveled. His first need was to go home.

The hen followed him willingly, and by eating and walking, eating and walking on again with due regard for caution, he at last came to familiar thickets and the blurring ox trace that was his uphill boundary line. He lifted his wings in silent preparation for his double clarion call, then beat them again in noisy drumbeat ruffle. Would there be a rival challenge? Had another cock come to claim this freehold in his absence? He listened, muscles tensed, but there was no answer. The glen was still his.

He led New Wife to a sheltered place where wind-toppled dogwood saplings made a latticed arbor over fern and bracken and left her to get acquainted with her new surroundings. She watched him for a moment, head a-tilt, compelled by unfulfilled motherhood to think of a nest site, even now when the normal brood time was long past.

The War Lord was following his usual survey route that would take him from corner to corner of his domain on crisscross trail. Now and then he stopped to give tentative churking query and at last he heard First Mate answer. She came stepping around an elderberry clump, her chicks hop-scotching behind her in their usual playful fashion, not at all concerned with their father's absence or return. For a few moments the cock and hen continued the low-voiced interchange, then the cock spied a caterpillar on humpback hunching across the grass and snapped it up to offer the hen as he had done in courtship. She accepted it, swallowing it at a gulp, and then seeing that her chicks were wandering off in a new game of Follow The Leader, she went clucking after them, and the War Lord resumed his patrol.

He had covered every corner now except the far stump lot where he had seen the boy with the gun, and he had not yet caught sight of Little Three's trio. The lesson he had learned there was already a part of his wisdom, but duty required him to check this outpost also.

The War Lord came into the clearing, every sense on the alert, and instantly saw the bold young cockerel whose daring had caused Little Three so much trouble that day with the hawk. The youngster still hadn't learned a shred of caution, it seemed, for he was running pellmell across the open space without once halting to look around, as if he had been called by a familiar and trusted guardian voice.

"Krrrukk!" called the War Lord in sharp reprimand. "Krrrukk!"

The chick did not even seem to hear him and all at once the War Lord saw the reason. He could hardly believe his own eyes and ears. It was the boy. The boy who had killed Little Three, and memory of the shape and sound of the weapon of death came back in redoubled image to the War Lord's senses. The boy was sitting on the same stump where he had sat before, but the searching eyes of the wary cock did not see the gun shape he remembered. Nor did the boy now have the glint-eyed hunter's look to him. Instead, he was calling to the cockerel in soft and coaxing tones and a rush of tumbling words.

"Chick. Here, little chick," Jed was saying. As he coaxed the cockerel to come to him, he thought of what his neighbor Tuck Hallowell had said the day Jed came home with the long-tailed hen. His grandfather and Tuck were in the midst of a checker game. Tuck had gawped at that long tail, Jed remembered with a chuckle, and gone off into a spiel about the birds coming all the way from China, packed off and paid for by some nabob named Denny, just because he liked the way they looked. Well, they were handsome. Jed had to go along with that. The one glimpse of the rooster had been enough to convince him that this was the handsomest thing in feathers any mortal was like to see, and he'd gotten his grandmother all excited at the idea of having gold and copper feathers for bonnet trim—till Tuck had spoiled it all by saying that there was a hundred dollar fine for killing the birds or even caging them.

A hundred dollars!

Jed could still feel the awful lump that came inside him at Tuck's announcing the impossible sum. Lucky for him the state legislature was still talking about the fine, settling the details and all, for ignorance of the law was no excuse and he'd have had to pay for the hen even if he hadn't meant to hit her, hadn't even seen her.

Now, coaxing the cockerel to him, he tried to explain once again—as he had every day since he began feeding the orphan chicks—that he had never meant to kill their mother. "Come, come eat," he coaxed again, scattering the grain.

Watching, the War Lord recalled the grain that had led to his own entrapment back in the almost-forgotten homeland. He called out renewed warning and saw that the chick again did not hear him. The youngster was head-down in the grain, gobbling so fast that bits flew out on both sides, and when he felt them patter on his own half-feathered body, he would leap aside with skittish air and then go back to eating again.

Now the boy was calling again, looking around into the bushes, and with his other hand tossing more grain, as if he expected the two timid sisters to appear also. The cockerel leaped away then, but when the boy was quiet again, he returned. Now the boy's hand reached back behind him again, and the War Lord could not hold back full-voiced warning.

"KKKKKRUK!"

This time the cockerel heard him, and flattened in prompt obedience, a blurred blob between the boy's boots, not understanding that the wearer of those boots was the very danger he had been warned to flee.

Now the War Lord repeated his alarm signal in still louder cry, and the boy sprang to his feet, shading his eyes to see more clearly. At the first arm movement, the cock leaped into the air for instinctive high-flight to the nearest tree, and then suddenly remembering how death had followed his mate here in this very place, plunged quickly into the weeds again, and stretching out till he was scarcely thicker than a blown leaf, went slipping through the sheltering stalks and stems. But he still felt need to repeat his warning for the foolish cockerel, and now he suddenly took to the air again with loud and noisy rattling of quills—the

91

delaying tactic that had caught his enemies by surprise before and might do so again, giving the chick a last chance for escape. He was giving himself a chance for escape, too, using full burst of speed to put leafy branches and thick trunks between himself and the lifted arm he thought held a gun.

But no gun blast came. The cock listened, then warily began reconnoitering return in search of the cockerel.

The youngster had at last taken proper refuge behind a stump under a twisted vine, frightened out of his wits when the boy had leaped to his feet to stare after the cock.

"He's back. The China bird came back!" Jed was whispering exultantly, spirits soaring beyond dreams with the cock's return and the thrill of having the cockerel eat from his hand for the first time. If only he hadn't jumped up like that, scaring them both—

Well, he had—and there was no use hanging around. Tomorrow he could try again. Maybe the little hen-chicks would come tomorrow, too. But he looked at the grain he had tossed for them under the bushes and saw that it had not been touched. They had never come out into the open to eat, like the cockerel, but they had always come to the grain they could eat without leaving the bushes. Had they been killed in the night by some owl or bobcat? Or were they just hiding?

Before he had seen the cock, Jed had been ready to accept the unhappy truth that the little hens had made some prowler a meal, but now the cock's return made any other miracle all the more possible, and so he convinced himself that they were only hiding. No use hunting for them. Not when he could hurry home and tell his grandmother the big news of the adult China bird's return and the even bigger news that the little bird had fed from his hand, would maybe come and feed from hers, too. She just couldn't get over talking about how far they'd traveled.

"China!" she'd say, shaking her head. It was the only place she'd ever made seem farther away than her old home in South Carolina, Jed thought.

"Chick!" he made one last call. "Here, chick!" But he didn't really expect the frightened bird to return, and he was off now in a hurry, not looking behind to see the little cockerel come after him at headlong scurry, one fear offsetting the other as he remembered now that his sisters were gone, his mother dead. The cock had returned only to take off again on rattling flight. There was no one left to follow but the boy.

Jed went bounding across the glen and through the woods, jumping over any stump or bush that got in his

93

way, feeling almost as if he could fly. He could just see himself coaxing the young bird to follow him. Already the feathers showed some of the cock's coloring and he'd have full plumage before too long, probably. Then how grand it would be to come walking up to the door, a full-grown cock beside him, and say to his grandmother, "Well, ma'am. Here's the far-come China bird to see you!"

He was so carried away by the vision that he could not stay earthbound one moment longer and went leaping up to catch the bough of a maple tree overhead for a dizzy skin-the-cat whirlover. Up, over and around he sailed, and then came down for thumping flatfooted landing.

A sickening squawk and crunch beneath his boots came to him with disaster warning, and he jerked away, looking down in horror at the crushed body of the cockerel.

He felt his stomach churn, bringing nauseous bile into his mouth, and gulped it back not able to believe what he saw. But the crushed body was there, silent accusation of his carelessness, and he bowed his head in a blur of tears, kneeling to scoop up the poor little lifeless blob.

From a distance the War Lord watched, seeing, but not understanding what he saw. Nothing he had ever

94

known could help him interpret the unbearable grief that whitened Jed's face as the boy realized the heartbreak cost of his own carelessness. Remorse has no place in wildling pattern, and even the mourning for the death of mate or young comes but briefly, as a rule.

But the inner command for survival is ever present, and in obedience to its law the War Lord saw only that in this place where death had come in strange and terrifying guise to Little Three, death had come also for the cockerel—and both times the boy was to blame.

No ruse the cock had ever learned, not even the age-old law of pheasant-kind to fly from a foe that came afoot, had helped save Little Three. The only safeguard was to go away from the boy and from the place —go away and stay away as far as possible.

That night the War Lord led New Wife and the reluctant First Mate and her brood to a roosting place at the farthest limit of his claim.

PART III

THE WANDERING

1

If the night had been warm and windless, as autumn nights can be in the northwest or anywhere when the time called Indian Summer is at hand, the War Lord might have slept soundly and wakened refreshed, his fears of the boy and the place of death screened over by lulling sense of body comfort. But it had not been warm, and there was a wind, an ice-born, chill-to-the-bone north wind howling down from Alaskan tundra and Arctic snowfields. As each new and colder air current swept over him, the War Lord wakened, ruffled his feathers in protest and was reminded afresh of discomfort and of the reason for his being in this unaccustomed place.

In the morning the compulsion of withdrawal was still upon him. To the east and west lay mountain barriers—the Coast Range and the Cascades—both heavily forested, and the ringnecks are not forest dwellers. They find food and nesting site in grasslands and brush country, at a forest's edge but not deep within tall-tree darkness. So the choice of route lay either north or south, and with the north wind still blowing its winter forecast, heading southward was inevitable.

An autumn migration to far southlands is not a part of inherent pheasant pattern, as it is with birds that do not have sturdy feet for scratching through crusted snow to get at hidden seeds and grasses. Yet even in temperate zones, the snow of the high country can come too deep for mere scratching aside, and so through ages past the birds of the pheasant clan had formed the custom of leaving the foothill meadows each autumn and journeying down to the warmer valleys where food was more easily obtained. Downward route, not southward, was where the needle of their inherited compass pointed, and now the downward slope took the War Lord from south to west, turning toward the river.

New Wife came willingly at his side, for the land was all strange to her and she was simply a follower with neither nest nor eggs nor chick to urge contradicting loyalty. First Mate was not so easily persuaded, and since her gangling young were still given to laggard games of jump-on-the-rock or run-around-the-stump, she turned laggard also, merely to keep them in her sight.

The War Lord was indulgent of these delays, since

there seemed plenty of good foraging on every side and he had no goal in mind to urge a faster pace, to accomplish any given distance by nightfall. But he was unusually alert for danger, and after the terrifying experiences of the past days, danger meant most of all the presence of men, and he kept well away from any sign of barns or houses, any sound of ax or saw or shouting voices.

First Mate and the chicks did not feel the same restraint, and now when they came to an abandoned wheatfield left to weeds and thistles when the inept owners had gone back to easier city living, they fell to gleaning with eager beaks, not heeding the command to move along. Unseen by even the War Lord, a gaunt gray cat crouched nearby under a weed tangle where she had been hungrily awaiting a careless sparrow, for the farm family had left her behind, having no need for a mouser in the city and not caring whether the cat could survive on her own. Now on stealthy belly slink she came after one dawdling chick that had been tempted on a foray of his own by a yellow butterfly, and as the cockerel leaped at the beckoning yellow wings, the cat leaped for the bird.

With a wing whir and war cry, First Mate was launching herself at the cat, for the butterfly had caught her eye, too, as she glanced up in accustomed between-bites survey, and by merest chance she had seen the slinking, gray-fur shadow. If the cat had been in her prime, well fed and lithe of muscle, First Mate would have been too late. As it was, the cat got a mouthful of feathers and might have dared for a second mouthful of something more nourishing if the War Lord had not come sailing back in full cry.

By the time he got there, of course, the cat had vanished, and now the chicks were quite willing to hurry along as the War Lord advised. They went on down slope at good pace, seeing the glint of flowing water ahead of them and feeling a reassurance at being once again at familiar water's edge.

But the river, when they finally reached it, was not much like the shallow, pebble-filled stream that had trickled down their old glen with only the overflow allowed by the horse rancher's dam. This was the Willamette, a working river, with log rafts and barges and river steamers. And they had chanced to come out just above an upstart river town with a new sawmill to add its own noisiness to the general hodgepodge sounds of human occupancy that had become the War Lord's most insistent danger signals.

He turned away from the town and might even have gone back the way he had come if darkness had not fallen upon them so suddenly, hastened by a bank of westering storm clouds. The pheasants needed shelter, and quickly. Even the hardy gulls were giving up their squabbling over the scraps on the town's trash heap and were heading across river in slim-winged flight for some unseen roost on the farther bank. A pair of crows were following the gulls, their black outline and plodding flap-beat gait in marked contrast to gull whiteness and easy gull glide.

The pheasants eyed them questioningly, for in a strange place the behavior of other birds could give welcome warning, and the flight of both crows and gulls to the far bank might be an indication of some unseen danger here on the shore they left behind. So long a flight was not customary for birds of the pheasants' bulk and short wing span, but it was not impossible, if there were need.

Then from a highwater tangle of stumps and willow roots on the bank just beyond came the reassuring and familiar buzzy trill of a towhee, and the pheasants turned toward it. This bird in jet-black hood and back, white front and rufous side panels was always one of the last to bed as well as the first to rise. It was a ground feeder, like themselves, and sought the same sort of thicket for nest and night shelter, and though they had never seen it in the old homeland, here in Oregon it had been a daily companion.

103

Now, joining with the towhee trill came the sleepy serenade of a song sparrow, and the pheasants needed no further assurance that all was well.

"K-ruk," said the War Lord, leading the way to the towhee's highwater fortress, and while the black-hooded songster flitted away to the brush to scratch for one last nightcap mouthful, the pheasants settled down on whatever snag or branch or hollow offered itself, tucked weary heads into ruffled feathers, and slept.

2

They were wakened next morning by the sound of approaching footsteps, low voices, and a spattering of pebbles that came bursting upon them with the force of full-flung aim. The youngsters were on their feet at the first clatter, ready to run for the open, but the War Lord gave muted caution, setting example with his own fast-freeze pose. This was not the first time he had lain motionless in a thicket while hunters chunked pebbles at his screen of tangled branches, and he had learned that men were usually discouraged by silence and went away.

But these men were not going away. They were coming closer. And with them was a dog. The birds could hear its heavy breathing, the whuffling of its flared nostrils as it caught their scent, then the sudden sharp-cut silence that meant it had gone into stiff-tailed freeze itself, to reveal their presence.

"Put 'em up, Rouser!" a man's voice bellowed, and as the dog lunged at the thicket, the pheasants spewed out to right and left—gangling young, hens and cock all at once, and as the War Lord cleared the thicket he saw the man's arms lifting the same stick-shaped weapon that had brought death to Little Three even in midair, and with desperation lunge he veered away just as the terrifying noise came crashing after him. The hot knife of pain stabbed one wing, scattering a handful of Ming blue feathers, but the bullet had hit only a glancing blow and the War Lord righted himself, gathering all his strength now for survival flight to the river's farther shore.

Below him he could see the muddy water, with no sign of midway reef or sandbank for resting place. Behind him came the shouts of the hunters, but whether in triumph for a long-tailed trophy or in disgust or sheer excitement the War Lord did not know and did not try to reckon. Every ounce of nerve and will power was concentrated on keeping his wings to steady rhythm, for the cooler water of the river sent no earth-warmed air current billowing skyward for buoying updraft so that he might make the crossing on set-wing glide. Nor had he had time to climb high enough at the start to allow for easy sky slide, and he was so dangerously close to the water that the least buffeting from the changeable over-water breezes might tip him into its depths.

Now he heard something behind him, and jerked

around in alarm. But it was only the wind-ruffling of New Wife's feathers as she came hurtling behind him in fear-flight frenzy. And behind her came one of First Mate's youngsters—a pullet—trapped by Follow-the-Leader instinct into a journey almost beyond her strength. At the head of this small caravan, the War Lord flew on. More water lay behind them now than lay ahead, but the remaining expanse still seemed endless, beyond wing strength.

A sudden wind flurry ruffled the water, and the War Lord felt himself slip sideways, the tip of the wounded wing touching cloying wetness, and as he righted himself with determined pumping, he heard New Wife stutter in fright as she, too, knew the sudden wind-tipped plunge into cold wetness. She was out of the river somehow, her frantic flailing bringing her to his side, and behind them they both heard the little pullet splash down and sink beneath the waves. In a moment the little brown head was surfacing, and with the same desperate wing strokes she used for land take-off, she was thrashing at the water in awkward but effective swimmer's stroke, head bobbing back and forth as if it, too, added to the forward propulsion.

Without the War Lord ahead of her for guidance, she might well have given up, but there he was, coming down on set landing glide to rock-strewn shore, with half-soaked New Wife landing beside him, and the little pullet made one more lunging effort, felt slippery rock beneath one foot—beneath both feet—and she was on dry land at last, stumbling toward the others with bedraggled gait and bewildered air, scarce knowing what had happened.

The pullet flopped down beside the larger hen, her pale beak open at full gape, eyes closed, her wings still giving convulsive half-flap gestures that sent showers of spray from water-soaked feathers. For her the ordeal was over, and she took no further thought of precaution, but the War Lord was still on the alert. Now he glanced skyward, and his body tensed.

Dark against the morning blue was the unmistakable long-winged shadow of a hawk coming swiftly toward them. *Slink from danger that flies . . .* that was the law by which the pheasants had achieved survival. Yet that law was gauged for the cover of tall grasses and here on the beach there was not even one straggly clump to offer shelter or camouflage deception. To reach the high-water tangle further up the bank would have taken only one fast flight, if wings were at full strength, but even the War Lord had not quite recovered after the frantic river crossing, as the pain in his wounded wing gave prompt reminder. To be caught in the air or on the ground seemed his only choice for one dread moment, and then suddenly the War Lord's taut body relaxed. The hawk was neither accipiter nor falcon, but an osprey, and fish made up its sole diet, as long as anything in fins or scales was available. Only in severest hunger would it prey upon bird or mammal, and only against starvation would it feed upon carrion. Such is osprey custom the world around, and on all the waterways of the world small hunted creatures that dread the hawk have learned to know the crook-winged outline of the osprey and its coloring of dark above, clear white below, worn by no other birds of its four-to-six-feet wing span.

This fish-eater has the keen eyes of all the hawk and eagle clan and would never have turned aside from its midriver breakfast patrol if the frantic churning of the pullet's wings had not seemed to give the pattern of a school of fish swarming close to the surface to feed on insects, or else to escape the pursuit of some underwater foe—a larger fish, an otter, or mink.

Now it saw only the strangely long-tailed cock and two bedraggled hens making scrambling retreat for the underbrush, and with a course-changing shrug of its black-wristed wings it veered off and away to renewed midstream search. A moment later it spied a telltale silvery wriggle and with swift, feet-first dive soon had its breakfast in the firm grip ensured by its roughened sole pads and was off to the spike-topped fir that was its usual lookout post, not even giving the strange birds a backward glance.

It would not have seen them, even if it had looked, for the War Lord, New Wife, and the pullet were all hidden now by a sprawling heap of river-tossed flotsam caught by a thicket of vine maple, and the bright crimson of the maple leaves against dead-leaf brown and umber was camouflage for both hens and cock. They huddled together for warmth and comfort. New Wife made a few compulsive pecks at her bedraggled feathers and then let weariness win over cleanliness, for once, and joined the pullet in sleep. The War Lord's eyes closed, too.

They slept the day through, disturbed only for brief rousings by the murmurs and rustlings as small animals and birds came and went away again on their own food hunts. Late in the afternoon they were jarred into sudden wakefulness by the arrival of a sky-filling swarm of migrant swallows, tardily leaving their Alaskan nesting grounds and stopping now to feed on the millions of tiny insects hovering midair above river and shore —fuel for the still longer journey that lay ahead. The birds swooped and swerved, keeping up a constant twittering that added still further confusion, coming down to snatch up a beakful right in front of the War Lord's blinking eyes. Most of them were either violet-green swallows or the darker tree swallows, both with clear white breasts. But there were also barn swallows with rose-tinged breasts and deep-forked tails, and these were the ones with the farthest journey ahead to Peru, Chile, and Argentina, where custom of untold ages had sent them each winter and would bring them back north each spring. Not many small birds come even close to matching the barn swallows' seven-thousand-mile flight and only a very few larger sea and shore birds have a longer route—the Arctic tern, Baird's and white-rumped sandpipers, the golden plover—but the War Lord and his hens knew nothing of this marvel that marked the swallows' pattern. They could see very plainly, however, that the swooping birds were making a very good meal. The War Lord began snapping up a few insects himself, even before he stood up to give his feathers the thorough shaking and re-settling they badly needed, and soon all three were groomed again and feeding busily, going on from the shore to the more tempting array of weed patch and meadow that lay beyond the water's farthest flood reach.

When darkness finally made further foraging unprofitable, they found themselves near a small stream

111

of trickling depth flowing down to meet the wide Willamette, as the stream in the familiar glen had done, and although the sparse clumps of willows gave scant protection, they settled down for the night without alarm. The absence of men—no shouting voice or gunfire had been heard all day—lulled even the War Lord's alertness, and he did not hear the faint ripple of water as a passing mink caught their scent and slipped out of the stream and over the dew-wet grass. Sharp white teeth stifled the pullet's last squawk, and the War Lord and New Wife roused in terror to see the slithering brown-fur shadow disappear with its bulky prize. With one circling glance, the War Lord marked the tallest tree and he and the hen took off to its high-branched fortress, safe again from danger that comes afoot, but still shaken by the pullet's loss, renewed reminder of endless danger.

In the morning they fed at aimless wander, seldom going far from the stream, but presently it widened out into a pond where a beaver colony had built a dam and now the War Lord turned away from its marshy banks, seeking drier footing. For the most part New Wife stayed close at his side, but food was hard to find and for hunger's sake she began searching for herself. All at once the War Lord heard her clucking excitedly with the same food-call she would have used for her chicks, and he hurried through the underbrush to join her.

She was in a clearing—man-made with ax and scythe, working over the trampled circle left by winter-browsing flock of deer or elk—and at the far end a small cabin was fenced in by a wobbly line of hastily driven saplings with a rickety gate, now propped open at spraddle-legged invitation. On the ground in front of the gate was a scattering of grain leading back inside with tempting trickery, and stretching out toward the underbrush where New Wife was pecking away with rat-tat beat of beak to hard ground. The War Lord stiffened, alert for danger, but all he saw was a strange barnyard hen coming out from the bushes across the way to eat the grain with the ease of long custom. Another hen joined her. Neither one gave the two pheasants more than a brief glance, and neither seemed surprised when the wild birds came out cautiously to feed in their wake, following them toward the gate.

Behind that gate, towheaded Chrissie Larson watched the bright-feathered long-tailed birds, her blue eyes fairly sparkling in excitement. Fairy tales were her favorite reading, and now her easily-aroused imagination convinced her that this was the magic firebird, come to life right out of her storybook. It was all she could do to keep from rushing out to ask him for three magic wishes, but there was good common sense as well as fairy-tale dreams beneath those tow-head braids, and Chrissie knew that she dare not move until her mother's hens were back in the yard. She had left the gate open, so it was her task to coax them back. She'd done it before, and the trickle of grain always brought them home, but, oh, it took so long. If they didn't hurry up, her father would be coming home from the logging camp and she'd get a scolding sure, unless he was so amazed by the firebird that he forgot to notice the escaped hens.

That might be one boon the firebird would grant her without asking, Chrissie thought, gazing enraptured at the crimson cheek armor, crown plumes and gold-bronze body. Every feather—

Chrissie drew in her breath in a shuddering sob. One moment the firebird had been there just a step from the gate and the next he was in high-arch flight to the forest, his mate behind him.

"Come back! Come back!" she cried out, running after them with outstretched arms, but her father's voice in explosive protest behind her brought her whirling around to see him lowering the shotgun, his face white.

"I might have killed you," he scolded, clutching

her to him. "Won't you ever learn to look before you jump?" His wife had come to the cabin door now, and he gestured back to the woods. "You see them? What were they?"

"That was the firebird," Chrissie said. "The firebird and his queen."

And she would not be shaken from her belief in the magic birds, no matter what they said. And after supper when her mother set her to her daily stint on the crosswork sampler, Chrissie took up her needle willingly. As soon as she finished the alphabet and the row of numbers, she was going to add a cross-stitch picture of the firebird. She could copy the picture in the fairy-tale book, adding the colors she had seen with her own eyes, she decided happily. The magic bird would never come back, she was sure, but she would have his picture to treasure always.

"Will you help me mark the x's for the pattern?" she asked her mother. "Don't you think a firebird will be just beautiful?"

Over her head Carl and Anna Larson exchanged indulgent smiles, and as the weeks went on and the long-tailed birds were never seen again—and no one at the logging camp saw them either—both parents were almost ready to believe that the fiery colors of the cock had been only Chrissie's lively imagination.

"Must have been somebody's prize rooster," Carl told Chrissie, giving a teasing tug to her long blonde braids. "You're not the only one to leave gates open, you know."

But when Chrissie's grandmother came down from Portland to spend the Christmas holidays, she took one look at the just-finished sampler and exclaimed in amazement. "Why, that's a China bird!" she said. "One of those new Denny pheasants. I can tell by the long tail."

"The—the *what*?" demanded her son.

"Denny pheasant. I read all about them in the paper. And I'd met Mrs. Denny once over at your Aunt Maude's, so I was interested, of course. But I hadn't heard that any of them had been let out down this way. The Denny place is up by Lebanon, you know."

"What?" Carl Larson repeated, still not certain what she was trying to explain. So she had to start over from the beginning, making everything clear, winding up her tale with the report that the state legislature had passed a bill giving the birds full protection for five years—and for another five years after that, if they needed it—and setting a hundred-dollar fine for anyone who dared molest them.

"A hundred dollars!" Carl exclaimed, with a whee-yew whistle for emphasis. "Good job they took off before I could pull the trigger. Fastest birds I ever saw."

"They saw your gun," Chrissie decided. "That's why they flew so fast."

"Oh, come now," her father protested. "You can't tell me any fool bird is smart enough to know a gun, just like that, before I even get it to my shoulder, or. . . ."

He stopped, thinking it over. "They might at that," he conceded. "They just might. Any birds that can come all the way from China and make themselves at home, just might be smart enough for anything. You know what? I bet they'll get on like sixty!"

3

In an abandoned deeryard down at the end of Beaver Creek, the War Lord was not living the easy life that Carl Larson had claimed for him. He had lost New Wife the week before when she stepped into a hidden noose set by Jim Beartrack, one of the Indians who worked for Red Rydan at the nearby logging camp. According to Jim's stomach, meals at the camp were downright skimpy, and they'd been even skimpier since the regular cook quit and Red had brought an old Chinese back from Portland to take over. Yan Chau was a pretty fair cook, Jim had to admit, even if the other loggers didn't much like having a Chinese around, but he didn't seem to have any idea of how much a working man had to eat to keep his stomach from sinking into his spine. To make up for the lack, Jim had taken to having an extra meal of his own fixing, slipping off to the woods alone whenever he had the chance. The long-tailed bird had been tasty. If Red hadn't caught him eating it and fired him on the spot, he'd probably have gotten the cock, too.

118

The War Lord was unaware of the reason for his reprieve, but he knew that the dark-haired man with the quiet step had not come back to the clearing or the encircling woods. The small songbirds who shared the glen with him knew it, too, and came flocking in to feed on weed seed and thistle with contented twittering. Bluebirds with soft coloring to match earth and sky. Goldfinches, the males as drab as their mates now, in winter dress, and without the black cap of spring and summer plumage. The big black woodpecker with the fiery crest drummed an accent to the twittering from a big fir that had recently become a host to wood-boring beetles, and when the drumming had tunneled through to where the larvae were cached, the long, snakelike tongue went curling out even beyond beak length to lick up the insect morsels. When they were eaten, he hunted another tree.

This afternoon the War Lord had left the clearing, too, following the meandering course of Beaver Creek. There was a strange restlessness coming on him. It had been of increasing insistence ever since he had been alone with no brown-feathered mate at his side to guide and guard. Guiding and guarding was part of the pattern that bound him, and without the demands of leadership, he felt ill at ease.

A sudden movement on the rocks at the stream's

edge caught his eye, and he turned sharply for a second look, remembering the brown-furred creature who had robbed him of the pullet. But the flashing shadow had been made by feathers, not fur. A gray-feathered, bobbed-tail bird teetered uncertainly on the rock and then slipped into the water with easy grace, letting the ripples close over its head, forcing its way underwater with energetic wing flips till it found some insect on the gravel stream bed and came back up to the rock to eat it. Now it straightened and preened each feather, waterproofing them anew with oil from its own preen gland, and once more plunged into the stream. The War Lord turned away, finding nothing of marvel in the dipper's underwater feat, nothing to remember.

Now it began to rain, an enveloping mistiness that seemed to come from everywhere at once, and the War Lord left the streambank, seeking a more sheltered nook. But he had come out now on the land that Red Rydan's loggers had recently cleared, and what with tramping men, falling trees, and the ox teams that had hauled out the logs, few places of shelter had been left.

No men were working now, for Rydan had run out of money, as usual, and the crew had gone on to find another outfit, leaving only old Yan Chau in his cook shack to await the new men Red promised to send. One or two of the loggers had suggested halfheartedly that Yan come along, but he had been afraid to try. Chinese workers were not welcome many places, except for jobs no one else wanted, and with Red he was at least sure of kindly treatment. The cook-shack shelf still held a fair-sized sack of beans and a few tins with torn labels, so that he would not go hungry for a while, and he could always find roots or greens in the woods, perhaps snare a few birds, if he could remember how the noose had been made and set in boyhood days back in the old home far away across the sea.

Yan Chau sighed heavily. He would never see China again. He had forced himself to put every thought of the lost homeland aside, and now when he tried to remember about the noose, he could not bring the old ways to mind. But he had found a torn boot-lace left by one of the loggers, and it would make a snare of sorts. Better than nothing. And the handful of grain he had found in a feedbag tossed aside and forgotten by the teamsters might do for bait. No use asking if it would really work. It was all he had, and it would have to do.

The old man worked slowly at first, fumbling with the knotted lace, letting the slender sapling he had chosen slip from his fingers and fly up to slash across his withered yellow cheeks. But as he tried again, his fingers began to remember what his mind had forgotten, and now he began to sing. The high-pitched wailing notes had neither words nor tune. He was not even aware that they were not still in his mind, still part of his remembering, for once he had started to call up his treasure hoard of memories, he could not stop.

The War Lord heard the keening song, but somehow it did not frighten him as shouts or laughter would have done. The singsong wail did not come to him with the warning of men's presence, for it was not a sound that he had linked with men in these last weeks when men with guns had come to be the enemy he feared most. He came on over the trampled roadway made by the oxen, stopping only when he saw the hunched, blue-clad figure beside the thicket, the wrinkled yellow hands patting at dead leaves and grass to cover the noose, reaching finally for the grain.

Yan Chau looked up, and the grain dribbled through his trembling fingers as he stared, mouth agape. This bird in the path before him was not flesh and feathers, but mystic spirit. It was the magic feng-bird, the bird of promise and good fortune embroidered on rich men's silken robes and painted on thinnest porcelain. It was all China, embodied in mystic vision sent by his ancestors to bid him join them in the realms beyond. With yearning cry the old man threw himself prostrate, awaiting fire, thunder, mist, and meteor. . . .

Instead, there came rattling quills and war-cry challenge, and the old man peered out from beneath his fingers to see the cock sail off on wide-wing retreat. Surely no magic bird would be thus frightened by an old man, he thought. So, then, it was a real bird after all. But how did a Chinese pheasant get to Oregon? He shook his head, finding no possible answer. Feng-bird, real bird—how could he know? To be on fortune's good side, he released the noose, vowing to set no more traps for anything in feathers.

The War Lord did not rest till he was back in the familiar deeryard. But even here he did not feel at ease. There was another place that called him. A place where he belonged, where he had been with others of his kind, the trusting mates who needed his care and guidance as he needed their trust. He could not define the restlessness within him or the urging that sent him onward, but he knew that he must move on. Was it the south wind blowing up warm and fresh from tropic sea islands that turned him northward with steady tailwind persuasion? Or was it partly the meandering stream leading him down to the wide-flowing Willamette almost to the very spot where he and the hens had made weary landfall?

However the course was chosen, here he was at river's edge, and there on the far bank was the noisy river town with its busy sawmill, the screaming gulls and quarreling crows, the trash heap and the docks. There on the upstream shore were the open fields, with highwater tangle that had become a trap, but the War Lord's searching gaze saw no hunters today, for a river steamer was just nudging the wharf, and everyone in town not sick abed was there to greet her arrival.

The War Lord launched into the air on silent wings, since the less attention he called to himself the better, and he crossed the river at fast wing beat, angling well upstream and away from the wharfside hullabaloo.

He saw the very thicket where he and the others had found shelter on their last night together, but it did not seem sheltering to him now. He left it behind, at quick pace, then slowed to the cautious searching gait compelled by unfamiliar terrain. If he had walked here in this field before, fed at that weed patch, or hidden in the sheltering underbrush on either side, he did not feel any stirring sense of reminder or welcome. He found a blackberry thicket and slipped beneath its twisted branches simply because night had overtaken him and he was weary. In the morning he would go on again.

At midday he came to a place he knew—the wood-lot where he had first heard gunfire, seen Little Three plummet to earth in deathfall and learned that high flight from danger that walks afoot was not always safe measure. Then he had linked the place itself with this strange new way of death, but he had learned since that it was not linked only to one place, but to the men that carried it with them anywhere they chose to go. He had learned the shape of that weapon they carried, learned to recognize the first betraying move of lifted arm. Knowledge was his own weapon. He could once more walk here with wariness his guard.

Every sense alert, looking to the right, looking to the left, stopping to listen at the slightest rustle, he skirted the woodlot and came at last to the blurred ox trace that had once marked familiar boundary. Still at the same wary pace he climbed the rise and came to the rock where he had stood each spring and summer morning to proclaim his freehold boundary. That special clarion call had not come from his throat in months now, for the ringnecks do not dispute boundary rights in winter quietus when there is no rivalry for hens or home. Usually it is mid-March before they feel the urge to find a lookout post and send a challenge ringing down glen or hill, time after time and day after day. But the first call comes earlier in zones where

125

spring's lengthening days are sooner begun, and a sudden warm spell in January or February with bright sunshine after weeks of cold winds and gray skies can start the cocks to crowing as quickly as the returning snow clouds can send them back to winter silence.

The cock stepped now to the rock and felt his feathers ruffle gently to the warming touch of the southwest wind. Chinook wind, the early settlers on the Oregon coast had called it, because it blew up to the little settlement at Astoria from the direction of the Chinook Indian camp. In the wild currant bush just beyond him, the cock now spied a song sparrow, tail down, head thrown back, the streaked throat quivering to warbled roundelay. He sang all year, warm or cold, rain or sunshine, but on a day like this his lilting chant rang out like spring's own theme song. From somewhere in the matted undergrowth, the song sparrow's golden-crowned cousin took up the medley with wistful, three-chime grace notes in perfect down-scale spacing of mi-re-do. He was only a winter visitor here, making no claim to nesting territory with musical signpost, but he sang anyway, whenever he felt like it, though he might sing louder and more often when he returned to his nesting ground farther north.

The War Lord could do what he felt like doing, too, now and then. And what he chose to do at this moment was to lift his wings for preliminary ruffle, stretch out his white-collared, jewel-tone throat and send forth springtime's clarion challenge. He gave his wings the second and louder drumbeat ruffling, and then the whole fanfare sounded so good to him, felt so satisfyingly the right thing to do in the right place, that he repeated it full voice.

Now he listened for an answering challenge, and heard instead a rustling of footsteps on dry leaves, and saw the slender form of a yearling cockerel come out from behind the currant bush, head crooked in curious and startled survey. Instantly the War Lord hurtled toward him with fiery eye and furious intent to battle, but the yearling was not yet ready to try cockerel spurs against the War Lord's formidable spikes, and with one gasping squawk, it scuttled off into the undergrowth, neither bird aware that it was a son who fled, a father who stood victorious. One cock only was the law, and the time for fatherly protection had passed.

Triumphant, the War Lord crowed again, standing his ground with defiant air against all others who might challenge him, but there was no answering boast. Then he heard the soft rustling steps again, this time from somewhere behind him, and he turned to see the leaf-brown plumpness of a full-grown pheasant hen. First Mate was here. She had returned somehow to the glen where they had raised their first young.

She came toward him slowly, as if not quite certain, but now her pace quickened, and they began calling to each other with low-voiced churking. The War Lord looked about him, seeking some food to give her in guardian token, and spying a clump of chickweed, gay in new green leaf and bud, he called her to come and feast, to accept his bounty.

She was there beside him at once, nibbling obediently, and the War Lord took a few nibbles of greenery himself. But a different kind of hunger came to him with more compulsive demand, the need to reclaim his land, to step off every path and runway, slope and glen, from high lookout post to streambank and back again; the need to find drinking place and hiding place and dust-bath hollow, as he had found them before when he and the hens had first been brought here, strangers—or all but strangers—to each other, and strangers indeed to the unknown land.

First Mate was no longer a stranger, and the land was no longer unknown. Here in this green Oregon valley the War Lord had at last come home.